W9-CLV-470

ELSINORE

Books by Jerome Charyn

ELSINORE
THE GOOD POLICEMAN
MOVIELAND
THE MAGICIAN'S WIFE
   (Illustrated by François Boucq)
PARADISE MAN
METROPOLIS
WAR CRIES OVER AVENUE C
PINOCCHIO'S NOSE
PANNA MARIA
DARLIN' BILL
THE CATFISH MAN
THE SEVENTH BABE
SECRET ISAAC
THE FRANKLIN SCARE
THE EDUCATION OF PATRICK SILVER
MARILYN THE WILD
BLUE EYES
THE TAR BABY
EISENHOWER, MY EISENHOWER
AMERICAN SCRAPBOOK
GOING TO JERUSALEM
THE MAN WHO GREW YOUNGER
ON THE DARKENING GREEN
ONCE UPON A DROSHKY

ELSINORE

JEROME CHARYN

ASBURY PARK PUBLIC LIBRARY
ASBURY PARK, NEW JERSEY

THE MYSTERIOUS PRESS
New York · Tokyo · Sweden · Milan
Published by Warner Books

 A Time Warner Company

Copyright © 1991 by Jerome Charyn
All rights reserved.

Mysterious Press books are published by
Warner Books, Inc., 666 Fifth Avenue, New York, NY 10103.

A Time Warner Company
The Mysterious Press name and logo are trademarks of Warner Books, Inc.

Printed in the United States of America
First printing: April 1991

10 9 8 7 6 5 4 3 2 1

Library of Congress Cataloging-in-Publication Data

Charyn, Jerome.
    Elsinore / Jerome Charyn.
        p.   cm.
    ISBN 0-89296-361-1
    I. Title.
    PS3553.H33E55   1991
    813'.54—dc20   90-12931
                                                  CIP

ELSINORE

Early Retirement

1

He lived at the Copenhagen, a few blocks north of the Dakota, where John Lennon had been killed. From his tower Holden could see Lennon's memorial in the woods, Strawberry Fields, a dark mosaic of rocks, grass, and trees. He was a boy in the heartland of Queens when John had come riding out of Liverpool with Ringo, George, and Paul. Holden's education began with Sgt. Pepper. Each time he entered a new war zone in Atlanta or L.A., Holden couldn't stop thinking of Sgt. Pepper's Lonely Hearts Club Band.

Murder seemed to follow Holden. Killings were his neighborhood . . . and his vocabulary. Columnists and reporters wouldn't leave his life alone. A short profile appeared in some Manhattan rag.

There's something fabricated about Sidney Holden. He wears secondhand clothes. But Holden doesn't shop at Salvation Army counters. His jackets and ties once belonged to the late Duke of Windsor.

Do clothes make the man? Then Sidney Holden is a new kind of Manhattan prince. Does he keep a chair at the Four Seasons, next to Henry Kissinger's table? No. He dines at Mansions, where celebrities prefer *not* to be noticed. Was Jackie O. in attendance last week? Count Josephus, Mansions' owner and maître d', would never tell on his clients.

Holden is fond of ratatouille.

It was in Mansions' dining room that Don Edmundo Carpentier, high priest of the Cuban Mafia, was murdered several months ago, surrounded by bodyguards and other lords of the realm. A lone man dispatched Don Edmundo, one of the most feared bandits in town. That man walked into the restaurant and shot Edmundo Carpentier while he was finishing his soup. No witnesses ever came forth to identify the assassin. And no one's been indicted for the crime.

Yet all we ever hear about is Holden's name.

The woman he lives with is the daughter-in-law of the Queens district attorney, a powerhouse in all five boroughs. But there's bad blood between Holden and the D.A., Paul Abruzzi, who'd like his daughter-in-law returned to his Pulitzer Prize–winning son, playwright Rex Abruzzi.

What's the secret of Sidney Holden?

Other reports began to surface. In *Vanity Fair, People, Manhattan, inc.* Photographers snapped his portrait out on the street. He had to use a private exit at the Copenhagen. It was difficult for his darling, Fay. When her children visited, Holden would go downstairs in dark glasses and shop for toys. He liked the little girls, blond creatures who had more composure than Holden ever had. They swallowed the stickiest cakes without dirtying their fingers. They would pat the corners of their mouths with huge napkins that Fay provided. The girls wanted his autograph for their classmates. He was much more exotic than their dad. What was a Pulitzer Prize compared to their mama's boyfriend?

Holden could have tolerated dark glasses for an eternity. He couldn't go to Mansions anymore and sit with Count Josephus and his little gallery of kings. But Holden didn't care. He had his darling . . . and visits from the girls. Fay developed a stutter during her sixth month with Holden. She'd start to sweat. She'd return from the supermarket minus her hat. She'd leave her gloves in the elevator. She'd forget to button her blouse. And when he'd talk to her, she could barely pronounce his name.

"S-s-s-sidney," she said.

They no longer made love.

She'd cry whenever Holden would touch her. He learned to live without fondling Fay. He hardly went anywhere with her. He had a ping-pong table lugged up to his tower and put in the living room, hoping he'd get to bat around a little white ball with his darling and her daughters. But the girls were studying ballet at school. Ping-pong was beneath them. And his darling couldn't seem to concentrate on the ball. Holden got rid of the table, lent it to August, captain of the doormen at the Copenhagen.

August was concerned about his darling. And Holden realized that nothing happened inside the building without the doormen's knowledge. The Copenhagen was like a high-class penitentiary. And Holden was a prisoner with money in his pocket. But he was still fond of Captain August.

The captain's origins were as obscure as his own. August had come from Germany after World War II. He had the look of a starved child, though he was fifty and carried a load of flesh. He was a pilgrim in America, like Holden himself.

In the old days, when he was bumping people for Aladdin Furs, Holden would have recruited August as a spy. He'd had a network of spies, run by his father's former mistress, but the woman had become a casualty of Holden's wars.

"Mr. Sidney," the captain said, "there's a ruckus downstairs."

"August, I'm not a referee. Call the cops."

"We'd rather keep it in the building, sir. One of the porters has gone berserk."

"I can't help that," Holden said.

"He's locked himself in the basement, Mr. Sidney. Beaten up two of our best boys. He says he knows you."

"What's his name?"

"Matthew, sir. Matthew Greene."

"I never met a Matthew Greene."

But Holden capitulated to Captain August. He rode down the back elevator into the basement. He'd never been to the basement before. It didn't have hammered-steel designs on the walls. It didn't have mirrors. But it had rooms filled with storage trunks from the time when Copenhageners of sixty years ago traveled by sea. The trunks were in beautiful condition. Holden had never seen this much burnished leather.

There were five rooms of trunks, and Holden had to wonder if sea voyages were coming back into style. He could have stored everything he owned in one of the trunks and still had room for himself. It was a marvelous way to travel.

Holden could have sworn he'd walked to the Bowery under the Copenhagen. His knees ached. He hadn't expected to join the infantry with Captain August. And then they arrived at a door. Nothing dramatic. A narrow door in the middle of a dark gray wall. And August knocked.

"Matt, he's here . . . I brought Sidney Holden."

But there wasn't any answer, and Holden had gone on a hike while his darling suffered upstairs.

"Please, Mr. Sidney . . . you talk to him."

Holden felt ridiculous, keening to a dumb door. "Matthew," he said. "It's me."

The door opened, and Holden ducked inside. He couldn't stand up straight in this room. It was some kind of utility closet. And Matthew Greene sat on a bench looking like a gnome. He was a short, wiry man with a shaved head. He had the aura of prison yards in his eyes, the taste of white bread and beans. Holden couldn't remember him.

"What is it you want, Greene?"

The little yardbird was holding a potato peeler in his

fist, and Holden didn't have to guess how sharp the peeler was. He was at the mercy of this little man.

"Did I bump your sweetheart?" Holden asked.

"Shut your fucking mouth," the porter said.

"And then what will we do? Eyeball each other until we starve to death?"

"Jesus, I was one of your rats."

"That's impossible," Holden said. "There were no Matthew Greenes on my payroll."

"I'm Kit Shea."

"I don't believe it," Holden said. "Shea had a full head of hair. He ran with the Westies. Shea wouldn't have been a porter, hiding in a closet."

The Westies had owned Manhattan as harbor pirates for a hundred years. But the unions had chased them off the docks. They couldn't compete with the twentieth century. They'd never organized. They sat in bars near the Hudson, murderous men who loaned themselves out occasionally. But they were too idiosyncratic to form strict family lines. They bumped and disappeared. Bumped and disappeared, and sat in their own graveyard. Kit was a little younger and more enterprising than the other Westies. He sold information. Much of it was no good, but having lived around such sad and doomed murderers, he could always tell if some Westie had been hired to take Holden's life.

"Kit, how'd you end up here?"

"It's a better cover than yours, Holden. I don't eat pickled carrots near the roof. And I didn't steal Paul Abruzzi's daughter-in-law."

"But I've never seen you in the building. And I've been at the Copenhagen nine, ten months."

"I make it my business to avoid the lobby. . . . I've heard the other porters. Sidney Holden, that's all they talk about. And his piece of ass."

"Don't say that. We're getting married."

"When?"

"The minute she divorces her husband. She'll get around to it. She hasn't been feeling well. What happened to you, Kit?"

"I had to punch out a couple of porters."

"Did they insult your mama?"

Holden saw the Hudson's bleakest water in Shea's eyes. "My mama's dead. . . . They were crowding me, Holden, coming into my shop."

"You have a shop at the Copenhagen?"

"Yeah. I make brooms in the closet. I do the handles. I tie the straw. I had my own lathe at Sing Sing. I made every fucking broom in the joint. I had citations on my wall, letters from the warden. They used to call me Michelangelo. And I caught two of the monkeys in the basement pissing on my straw."

"Couldn't you have told Captain August?

"I didn't have the time. I'm a Westie. I don't believe in arbitration."

"Where are those porters?"

"Captain sent them home to convalesce."

"Then why don't you come out of the closet?"

"Because Captain also sent for the cops. They're sitting in the lobby, Holden. And I have too much of a reputation, too much of a past. I'm not going back to the joint. This is Kitty's closet. Kitty don't budge."

"August didn't send for the cops."

"I don't believe you," the broommaker said, clutching

his peeler. And Holden understood that little Shea was waltzing at some kind of edge. He needed the Hudson. All Westies were river rats.

"Come upstairs, Kit."

"Make me, paradise man. Go for your gun."

"I'm not carrying a gun."

"That's a laugh," Kit said.

"My picture's all over the place. I took early retirement."

"The government's paying you not to slap people. Wish I could afford social security like that. . . . Holden, leave my country, huh? Leave my house."

But Holden felt responsible for his rat. He didn't duck out the door. And Shea drove the potato peeler toward Holden's neck. Holden couldn't swing his arm in that narrow closet. But he could make a fist. He didn't worry about perimeters. His fist moved six or seven inches until it struck the underside of Kit's jaw. Little Shea rose up to the roof of the closet and fell into Holden's arms. He was still clutching the potato peeler, but he cut his own hand on the sharp edges.

Holden brought him out of the closet, took the potato peeler, and wrapped Shea's bloody fingers in a handkerchief that cost a hundred dollars.

He didn't reveal Shea's identity to Captain August. "Here's your Matthew Greene. But he thinks you have cops waiting for him in the lobby."

"He's insane. I wouldn't bring cops into the building."

Holden found a taxi for Kit Shea and went upstairs to his darling. She could have been another Shea, taller, blonder, with tits, but she had the Hudson in her eyes, depths of water where Holden couldn't reach.

"I'll fix you some ratatouille," she said, like a sleep-walker.

Holden chopped the onions, soaked the greens.

His darling had talked about supper and then wandered into the bedroom and closed the door.

Holden found little Shea's peeler in his hand. He struck at a carrot and almost started to cry. He was like a child in his father's house, bewildered by the world. But his father was dead. Holden prepared the vegetables and made ratatouille in a pot.

He lit a candle and called his darling in to eat.

"Fay . . ."

"I'm not hungry," she said. She sat curled on the windowsill, with Strawberry Fields behind her back. And Holden was left to eat with Sgt. Pepper's Lonely Hearts Club Band.

2

He had an office, a great big room at the Aladdin Fur Company that had once served as his living quarters. He would walk down to the fur district, but there was nothing to do. The market was filled with Greeks. They were frightened of Sidney Holden, but they liked to pat his sleeve, touch Holden, feel his fame. Aladdin employed no Greeks. The cutters and nailers were from a lost generation, before the Greeks monopolized the market. They knew how to dress a mink. They were masters in a trade that had no stability at all. Half the coats they cut were already out of fashion. Holden had no instinct for dark skins on a board. He would pick up his check, nibble on a sandwich, and run.

He couldn't threaten people who owed Aladdin money. It would have been like the bark and bite of a tin man. He was too famous. The people he threatened would only ask him for his autograph. So he went to his office once a week, for half an hour. He didn't talk on the telephone. He sat and considered whatever future he might have.

He was in the middle of a reverie when the phone rang. No one called him at the office anymore, not Fay or his senior partner, Bruno Schatz, the Swiss, who controlled the Paris end of Aladdin's operation. Swiss was a wise man . . . and a thief. He swindled half the world and hid inside Aladdin's label. Aladdin was the cover for all his mischief and mayhem. Schatz was eighty-one. And the lines of his future were much more clear than Sidney Holden's. Schatz was married to Holden's wife, Andrushka. Andrushka was a bigamist. She'd never bothered to divorce her little Sid.

The phone stopped ringing, then started again. Somebody wanted Holden. He picked up the phone, but he didn't hear that familiar static of a Paris call. It couldn't have been Schatz.

"Hello?"

"Am I talking to Mr. Sidney Holden?"

A woman's voice, cultured and sweet. She didn't sound like the candy stores of Queens, where Holden spent his boyhood chewing chocolate sundaes.

"Yes, this is Holden."

"I'm Mrs. Vanderwelle, Gloria Vanderwelle. I represent Mr. Phipps of the Phipps Foundation."

"I'm sorry, Mrs. Vanderwelle. I'm not familiar with foundations."

But it was a lie. He'd heard of Phipps, the billionaire philanthropist who was much older than Bruno Schatz. Ninety and he walked to work. Holden had read that in *Manhattan,inc.*

"We finance social projects, Mr. Holden . . . hospices

for people dying of AIDS, apartments for the homeless, clinics for battered wives, and music classes for gifted children who can't afford a violoncello. . . ."

"But I'm not a philanthropist, Mrs. Vanderwelle. I mean, I could contribute to one of the causes."

"This is no solicitation, Mr. Holden. Mr. Phipps would like to meet you."

"Are you his secretary?" Holden asked.

"I'm his lawyer," she said. "And I direct the foundation."

"I still don't understand."

"We would like to hire you, Mr. Holden."

Ah, they wanted him to bump another philanthropist.

"Mrs. Vanderwelle, I can't afford to auction my services, understand? My fiancée is sick. I appreciate the phone call, but . . ."

"Shall we say ten o'clock tomorrow morning, Mr. Holden? A late breakfast at the foundation . . . or an early lunch."

And before he could tell her no, the bitch had hung up on him. How did she get Holden's line? It wasn't listed.

He walked out and locked the door.

He didn't find much comfort at the Copenhagen.

Fay was gone.

The building was cluttered with shooflies from the Queens district attorney's office, detectives in pink socks who carried Fay's wardrobe in their arms, skirts, dresses, underwear. They smiled, and they had the key to his apartment. He wrestled with the shooflies in front of the elevator door. There were five of them, and they had blackjacks. But Holden had one advantage. The vestibule was small. They couldn't clutch Fay's wardrobe and also swing their arms. He leapt into the five of them, and they landed on the floor in a bundle of clothes, like some great cotton ball.

The elevator opened and Paul Abruzzi stepped onto the landing. The Queens D.A. had to mince about in his black shoes until his men extricated themselves and stood with their shoulders squeezed against the wall. He didn't seem angry at Holden. He was a man of sixty-one who wore baggy suits and had silky white hair. Paul didn't have Holden's tailor. Holden's tailor had swiped the patterns of kings and several dukes.

"Morons," the D.A. said to his shooflies. "I didn't ask you to feel her underpants. Get out of here."

They boarded the elevator and Paul Abruzzi let himself into Holden's apartment. Holden had to follow him inside. There were no introductions from Paul, no polite talk about Holden's sudden fame in the republic of Manhattan.

"Sidney, I have a court order . . . I have a writ."

"Show me," Holden said.

Paul produced a scroll with the seal of New York. It was signed by a judge. Paul could get a writ anytime he wanted. He owned the courts.

"It's still a fucking seizure."

"The woman is suicidal, or haven't you noticed?"

"I've noticed, Paul. I've noticed. But you picked a convenient time. I'm gone two hours, and you come around with your writs. You staked the house, didn't you? You had your shooflies in the park, wearing camouflage suits."

"Does it matter, Sidney? You don't have a legal claim on the woman. She wasn't your wife."

"And you? The father-in-law who romanced her away from your own son."

"Are you going to be tiresome, Sidney? I wanted to behave like a gentleman with you."

"Where is she, Paul?"

"That's privileged information, son."

"I'm not your son. Your son writes plays with his dick in his hand."

"But he's responsible for her, Sidney, not you. As far as Fay is concerned, you don't exist."

"I'll find her," Holden said.

"I'm sure you will. But if you go near her, if you force your way in, you'll never leave the place. The guards I hired have your photograph from *Vanity Fair*. They've been trained to kill."

"I'm a bumper, Paul, or did you forget?"

"Those days are over."

Paul started to leave. Then he turned to Holden. "Didn't I tell you the crying spells would start? It's like a fever. She crawls into a depression and she can't crawl out. She was better off with me. She didn't have to worry about true love."

"I'll find her."

"Good-bye, son."

He had lunch at Fine & Schapiro, where John Lennon liked to eat in dark granny glasses. Lennon would sit at the back of the restaurant, undisturbed. Holden had half a chicken in a pot. He had soup with special little soup nuts. He had half-sour pickles. He signed his autograph on the waiters' menus. If he meditated long enough, he might meet Lennon's ghost.

He sat at Fine & Schapiro through lunch and dinner. He made three telephone calls. He had more soup nuts.

Finally, at ten o'clock, as the waiters were stacking chairs, a short, thick man entered the restaurant. His skin looked as if it had been waxed by a mortician. He dressed like a ponce. He wore a purple jacket and gold rings and a toup that seemed stuck on his head with mustard plaster. He was a retired police captain named Brian Calendar, who'd once worked for Paul. He ran a detective agency near the Queens Criminal Court Building. He was the best bloodhound Holden had ever used. And he hated Paul. Paul had forced him to retire. Calendar was an extortionist and a thief, but he was also reliable.

His hands trembled. He had Parkinson's disease. He ate a bowl of half-sour pickles. His eyebrows and his mustache had been dyed a rich, silky black. Holden didn't have to explain a thing.

"Paulie took back the merchandise."

"He kidnapped her," Holden said. "He's got her in some fancy snakepit."

"A sanitarium?" Calendar asked, his eyebrows crinkling in separate directions, as if whatever motor he had could only master individual parts.

"Yeah, a sanitarium."

"Holden, there's fifty states. And that doesn't include Switzerland."

"But he has a weakness for her, Brian. He wouldn't stick her far away."

"True," Calendar said, eying the soup nuts in Holden's bowl. "What's that?"

"Soup nuts."

"Never heard of such a thing. . . . Waiter, I'll have some of that, in a big bowl."

But Fine & Schapiro had been around for fifty years, and the restaurant didn't have to rush for a private detective with Parkinson's disease.

"Sorry, the kitchen's closed," the waiter said.

And Calendar got up from the table. All the trembling was gone. He was a police captain again. And the restaurant, with its salamis on the wall, could have been his own lost precinct. "Soup nuts," he said.

The waiter scampered into the kitchen and returned with a tureen of soup.

"Thanks," Calendar said. "I don't need a bowl." He served himself with an enormous ladle. "We were talking about Paul."

"You know his habits," Holden said. "And the safe houses he would use."

"If a judge signed the commitment papers, Paul could never use a house of his own. Did you look at the writ?"

"I saw it, but I didn't really look."

"Ah, it could have been a phony document. And it wouldn't matter. He'd have her switched half a dozen times, just to fuck you in the head. But I'll have a peek at the records, Holden. There's always a clerk I can kiss. Don't worry. I'll find the princess. But it will cost you five K. In advance."

"Brian, we're not sitting in a vault. I wouldn't carry that much cash around."

"Gimme what you got."

Calendar took his change, and his small bills, everything Holden had in his pants. He drank the soup from
the tureen and belched once. Then his hands started to
shake, and Holden began to have some doubts. But
Calendar was the closest he could get to Paul.

Holden sat another half hour while the restaurant
went dark. He couldn't see his own face in the mirror.
He dreaded going home.

No one chased him from the restaurant, and he didn't
need cash. He had a charge account at Fine & Schapiro.
He walked out a little before midnight. He had two
beers at the Irish bar across the street. A woman kept
staring at his clothes. She had a bruise under her eye.
Battered wife. Holden could have introduced her to the
Phipps Foundation.

"Mister, that's one hell of a suit."

"It belonged to the Duke of Windsor once upon a
time."

"How did you inherit it?"

"My tailor had it swiped from the Duke's closet."

"You're a lucky man to know," she said, putting her
hand inside Holden's sleeve. "My name's Irene."

"Who hit you?" Holden asked.

"Some guy . . . but he's out of the picture. Say, aren't
you Sidney Holden? Could you come upstairs and beat
the hell out of my old man?"

Holden paid for the beers with a credit card and left
without Irene.

It was almost two o'clock when he arrived at the
Copenhagen.

His telephone rang a minute after he opened the door.
It was Paul Abruzzi.

"Don't you ever sleep?" Holden asked.

"Sidney, you're a bad boy. You shouldn't have hired that scumbag. I had to put him in the tank. Brian was carrying a couple of unlicensed guns."

"Paul, let him go."

"That's up to you. . . . Here, I'll put him on. We can have a conference call."

Holden waited and then Calendar said hello. He was crying. "I'm sorry."

"That's okay, Brian."

"Tell him," Abruzzi said.

"You'd better stop looking for Fay."

"Tell him again."

"Don't look for Fay."

Holden hung up.

He slept in the living room because he couldn't bear to lie in his own bed without Fay. He didn't really sleep. He crept around like a forest animal, watching the lights of Central Park. A somnambulist in silk socks.

3

He never showed at the Phipps Foundation.

He couldn't stop thinking of Fay.

The other bloodhounds he knew wouldn't return his calls. Paul was a very good teacher. No one wanted any sort of job from Sidney Holden.

"I'll find her myself," he said. But he couldn't seem to get off his ass. He visited Strawberry Fields, saw the mosaic Yoko had put in the ground, with the word, "Imagine" in the middle. He'd come out of his own Liverpool, but he didn't have John's genius. He was almost thirty-nine, and he felt like a hundred and six.

A week passed and he went to Aladdin again. But there was no check in his mail slot. None of the nailers or cutters would have dared rip him off. They couldn't break a check into peanut brittle and have it disappear in their mouths. He walked into his office and dialed the Swisser, Bruno Schatz. He couldn't get through to Paris.

The phone rang, and Holden figured that the operator

had found Schatz. But it was the lawyer lady. Gloria Vanderwelle.

"Are you always such a delinquent, Mr. Holden? We had a breakfast date."

"I told you, Mrs. Vanderwelle. I'm retired."

"Mr. Phipps still wants to meet you."

"Look," he said. "My fiancée was kidnapped. I can't sleep. And I couldn't concentrate on breakfast. I'll meet him next month, okay? I promise. I'll sit and eat croissants."

"Will tomorrow at ten be satisfactory?"

"Don't you ever listen, Mrs. Vanderwelle?"

"Mr. Phipps is a compassionate man. And he has splendid resources. He doesn't like lovers to be apart. He'll get you to your fiancée."

"Is this a gimmick, Mrs. Vanderwelle? Because if the old man is romancing me, I wouldn't—"

"He's not an old man. We'll expect you at ten. And please wear a tie, Mr. Holden. It is a foundation."

He wore Windsor's tie, Windsor's shirt, and Windsor's jacket to the Phipps Foundation. Phipps had his own building on Park and Thirty-ninth. It had marble on the floors and metal beaten into the walls. The ceiling looked like some constellation of silver stars.

The foundation occupied a single floor, but the rest of the building was also devoted to Phipps. Phipps Bookbinding Corporation; Phipps Metalurgical; Phipps Tool and Die; Phipps Entertainment Industries. It was like a vertical country, where Phipps was landlord and king.

Holden went up to the foundation. A receptionist sat

behind a glass cage, and Holden wondered if it was bulletproof. She stared at his Windsor Special. He could have waltzed out of another age, where men had all the elegance of a handsome, muted line.

"I'm Holden," he said. "I have a breakfast appointment with Mr. Phipps."

She pressed a button, whispered a few words, and said, "Have a seat."

But Holden didn't like to sit in outer offices. He didn't like to sit at all when he was wearing his Windsor, because bending his knees ruined that flawless line.

He looked at the photographs on the wall, photographs of foundation projects. A room of battered wives; an ugly boy with a violin; a recreation hall of dying men. It seemed to Holden that the Phipps Foundation drew calamities to itself. But he was glad of it: there was nothing buttery on the wall, nothing meant to reward or inspire. It was like the spaces Holden had lived in, in spite of Windsor's suit.

A woman came out of an inner office with a bow in her hair. She looked twenty in her tinted eyeglasses. Holden figured she was some messenger girl, an intern from one of the Catholic colleges. Perhaps a student nurse. She was a bit shorter than Holden. She shook his hand. And when she smiled, he knew she wasn't a nurse.

"I'm Mrs. Vanderwelle."

Holden looked again. "You can't be more than twenty-five."

"I'm thirty," she said.

"But you run this operation."

"Yes, Mr. Holden. I've been around. I graduated from Harvard Law when I was nineteen."

He couldn't decide if she was pretty or not. She didn't have Andrushka's long legs or Fay's curly hair. She wore a suit, like Holden, but without a tie. Her perfume dug into Holden a little. He expected to see her on the walls, with a violin in her lap. Foundation Graduate, Gloria Vanderwelle, All-American Girl. But then he remembered that Vanderwelle was her married name.

She led him into a corner office that was laden with glass. It had the perfect pinch of Manhattan. Holden could see both rivers from those glass walls.

The old man was behind his desk. Holden was disappointed, because Howard Phipps wasn't wearing a tie. He had a shirt open at the collar and a cardigan with patched sleeves. He didn't get up when Holden entered the room.

Holden looked for Gloria, But she'd slipped out with that bow of hers, and the bumper felt uncomfortable. He'd never talked to a philanthropist or a billionaire. But then Phipps turned to look at him. There was a hardness around the eyes, a strictness to the cheeks. And Holden understood. Howard Phipps was a bumper too. It didn't matter how many hospices he'd built, or virtuosos he'd thrust upon the planet. He'd had people killed. That's why he'd wanted Holden in the house. So he could talk bumper to bumper.

"Holden, would you care to sit?"

"Thank you, Mr. Phipps, but I prefer to stand. I like watching both rivers."

"Should we have breakfast now?" Phipps said, like a kindly doll in his cardigan. If he was ninety, Holden couldn't tell. He had no liver spots or wattles under his neck. His hands didn't shake, and he didn't have Calendar's waxen look.

"Is this the breakfast room?" Holden asked.

"No. We'll run upstairs to the restaurant. But I'll be blunt. I purchased your contract six days ago."

"I'm not sure what you mean."

"I own Aladdin Furs."

"You bought out Bruno Schatz?"

"Entirely."

"And I was never notified? I'm vice president."

"That was window dressing," Phipps said. "You were never really an officer of the corporation."

"I'm speechless," Holden said. "A vice president, and I'm shunted out the door, like a bag of garbage."

"Here," Phipps said, and he handed Holden his check, signed by Howard Phipps, president of Aladdin Furs.

"But it's a dying operation," Holden said. "The Greeks own more than half the market. What would you want with a load of minks?"

"I wanted you."

"I don't understand," Holden said. "I'm not so valuable that you had to buy a whole company out from under the Swiss. If you needed a favor, why didn't you ask?"

"I did. But you never showed up for breakfast."

"I was having problems with my fiancée," Holden said.

"Come, let's eat."

The old man got up from behind his desk. He was taller than Holden, but his back was slightly bent. Phipps walked with a cane. His shoes looked like rubber boats. But even with the cane he was almost as quick as Holden.

They rode upstairs in Phipps' elevator car and stepped out into a restaurant that was three stories high and had the tapered walls of a cathedral with cut glass and metal bands that circled the ceiling in narrowing lines. Holden figured they were near the roof. There were murals on the walls of a New York that belonged to an age Holden had never heard about. It was a city of ramparts and flying boats, where the streetlife seemed to exist on laddered walkways and terraces that could float. One of the murals had words beaten into the corner with gold.

MANHATTA 1988

And Holden realized what it was. An artist's dream of Manhattan fifty years ago, a futurescape of glass tendrils and concrete vines. A city dweller's idea of Jack and the Beanstalk. It was lucky that Holden had studied art and architecture with a graduate student from Yale. He'd been trying to keep up with Andrushka, a mannequin from the fur market who'd swallowed all of Cézanne after she'd married Sidney Holden. And now Holden wasn't lost in this environment. He could interpret crazy murals on the wall.

But he didn't understand the restaurant. It covered an entire floor like some mock battlefield with soldiers that were held in place. Holden counted two dozen waiters. They couldn't have come from Fine & Schapiro. They were tall and very blond and wore dinner jackets that Windsor himself wouldn't have been ashamed of. But there was no turmoil attached to them. The waiters didn't move. And it had nothing to do with any awkward hour between breakfast and lunch.

No one eats here, except the old man.

"You look startled," Phipps said.

"Was this place ever opened to the public?"

"Holden, it was the classiest spot in town. Took weeks to get a reservation. Even I had a hard time, and I owned it. That's how independent my managers were. 'Make him suffer,' they said. Garbo had a corner table. She loved to watch people dance."

"What was it called?"

"Something simple. I didn't care for those Parisian titles."

"Simple, but what?"

"The Supper Club," Phipps said. "That's all."

"And then . . ."

"I closed it down."

"Did you start losing money?"

"Of course not. And even if I did, I had a hundred offers to sell."

"What happened?"

"Let's eat," Phipps said.

"Any particular table?"

Phipps smiled. "Holden, we can eat wherever you like."

And Holden tramped among the tables with Phipps and decided to sit under a mural. It was like wandering into an orderly forest, where the waiters themselves were the animals and Holden the hunter, but he still didn't know why he'd come to hunt.

"What happened?" he asked while the waiters arrived with silverware.

"What always happens. I was in love. I brought her here every night I could. She was twenty. I was forty-five. And she was more of a woman than the grandmas at the other tables. I was the boy, Holden. I was the boy. Jealous. Petty. Stupid. I had a private army watching. They sat with her at lunch counters. She begged me to stop. 'Please,' she said. I read into that remark. I saw secret lovers. I doubled the detail of men and women who were following her. I collected all the notes, bound them into books. It was like a library of precise gibberish."

"I know what you mean. I get crazy when I'm in love. But couldn't you have stopped yourself, Mr. Phipps? Did your army come up with anything that could incriminate your girl?"

"Not a word."

"And that still wasn't enough?"

"No. I was the greedy sort."

Food appeared at the table. Bread, cheese, omelettes, apples, and a soufflé. Demitasse that was almost as delicious as the coffee in Rome, where Holden had done some piecework for Schatz. He had an omelette with grapes in it. The bread crumbled in his fist like cake.

"Even as I started to lose her, Holden, I was happy. I had a picture of her life, from moment to moment."

"But you're not happy now."

The old man ate his coffee with a spoon.

"It was inevitable. She ran away, married an accountant in Rochester. I wrecked his firm. He had no idea what was happening. The poor man committed suicide."

"And the girl?"

"Went out of her mind, Holden."

"What was her name?"

"Judith Church."

"She still alive?"

"Yes. She's a baby . . . sixty-seven."

"And you want me to find her? Is that what this breakfast is about?"

"Find her, man? I know where she is. You think I'd ever lose sight of her?"

"Did she recover her senses?"

"Of course," Phipps said. "The woman wasn't a lunatic. She was under distress."

"Why didn't you court her again?"

"Bloody logical, aren't you, Holden? I did court her again. She wouldn't have me. Said I'd ruined her life. Hated my smell. Hated the look of my face. But that's how I am. I manipulate. Stocks. Bonds. People."

"Where is she now?"

"Right in New York."

"And you want her back?"

"No, no. That's not the point of the story. We were talking about my restaurant. I shut it down after Judith went to Rochester that first time. I couldn't bear to watch people eating under this roof while she was away. I wanted to murder them all, the bloody bastards, chewing their steaks."

"That's a bit eccentric for a businessman. Why didn't you keep off the property?"

"I couldn't. I'd open my eyes and imagine her eating at a table with other men."

"I studied accounting, Mr. Phipps."

"I know. Three semesters at Bernard Baruch College. I had you investigated. I always do that when I consider hiring someone."

"You didn't let me finish," Holden said. "You were making a fortune from the place, right? You could have sold it, but you didn't want to. Then why didn't you come up to this joint wearing a blindfold, so you wouldn't have to imagine looking at your lady?"

The old man started to laugh and coffee dribbled from the edges of his mouth. A waiter arrived with an enormous napkin. Phipps seized it and patted his mouth. Then he returned the napkin and banished the waiter to some far corner of the restaurant. "I like you, Holden. I like you very much."

"I still don't understand what I'm doing here. I can't help you with your darling. I don't kidnap women, Mr. Phipps. And three semesters at Baruch doesn't qualify me for any of the outfits you run."

"You're valuable to me."

"How? If it's heavy-duty work, you could bribe the CIA or one of the new Mafia families. They could lend you a hand."

"That's not the kind of hand I need."

"Then what is it?" Holden asked, tiring of all that food on the table. The unobstructed depth of the restaurant was killing him. He'd come to a ghost city. Would the waiters disappear if he pricked them with a needle? Were they animated balloons from one of the workshops downstairs? A product of Phipps Enterprises?

"I'm ninety-two, Holden. I'd like a companion."

Holden looked at the old man's eyes. "If it's funny stuff, I'm not into that. I have a fiancée, even if I can't reach her at the moment." Holden stood up. "I think I'll say good-bye . . . and you can have your check back."

"Sit down."

"I like it better when I stand. I can watch all the murals."

"Sit down."

Holden sat.

"I'm sick of philanthropy . . . I want to get back into the life."

"I don't know what you're talking about."

"You know. That's why I need you. I can't go charging around all by myself."

"Then hire a nurse with a pair of guns. . . . Mr. Phipps, you're a little crazy. *The life. The life.* You want to handle cocaine? Be my guest. All you have to do is buy a little airfield and you're in business."

"I'm not interested in cocaine. I was thinking of funny paper."

"Oh, that's a lovely idea. Funny paper, when you've got billions of the real thing. No wonder Judith Church ran away. You're into scary projects . . . and why are you telling me all this? Are you so sure I'm not wearing a wire? I could be a rat for some federal prosecutor, waiting in line for the witness protection program. I could sink you, Mr. Phipps."

"Holden, I have dinner twice a month with the attorney general."

"All right, so you're bulletproof, but why me?"

"I trust you."

"We've never met. Are you telling me I have an honest smile, some shit like that?"

"I've known you since you were a boy."

"Stop that," Holden said. "I wouldn't forget a billion-aire."

"I never really introduced myself to you. That would have been indiscreet. We had ice-cream sodas several times."

"Where and when?"

"Jacobi's on Kissena Boulevard . . . I'd say nineteen sixty or 'sixty-two."

Holden felt a murderous beat in his forehead. "My father always took me there. It was out of the way. He'd drive me in his company car . . . between assignments for Aladdin Furs. He was Bruno Schatz's chauffeur."

"Sometimes Schatz lent your father out to me."

"That's impossible," Holden said. "My dad was under wraps. Schatz had to find him a new name and every-thing. He was an outlaw."

"You misunderstood. He didn't hurt anyone for me. Your father was my collection agent. And we'd meet at Jacobi's from time to time. I was fond of him . . . and his wife. A black woman."

"Mrs. Howard. They lived together. But they were never married."

"I wasn't being technical about it," Phipps said. "And we talked, you and I . . . at Jacobi's."

"What about?"

"Baseball, I think. Johnny Mize. And James Bond. You liked Double O Seven."

"Then it couldn't have been nineteen sixty. That was before *Doctor No*."

A hollow appeared between the old man's eyes. "Didn't I say 'sixty or 'sixty-two?"

They were silent for a moment, stuck in some little war game of years and ice-cream parlors. Holden still couldn't remember an old man asking him questions about Johnny Mize. But Holden Sr. might have talked to Phipps about Mize. His dad had been delirious about baseball.

Mrs. Vanderwelle had come upstairs with a message for the old man. She sat down at the table and Holden looked at the bow in her hair. He still couldn't decide whether she was pretty or not. She had a cup of coffee while Phipps signed a few documents with a leaky ballpoint pen. His signature covered half the page.

"Are you enjoying yourself, Mr. Holden?" she asked.

"Yes. I like the decor. And the service."

"Then you ought to come again." She got up, took the documents from Phipps, and walked to the elevator. Holden watched her rump. It was an enigma. He'd never met a woman he was so undecided about.

"I don't like the way you look at her, Holden," Phipps said. "She's off-limits."

"I apologize," Holden said. "It's just that I can't picture her as the head of a foundation. And if she's your personal lawyer, she must have an awful lot on her mind. Does she do criminal work? If you're going to become a bandit at ninety-two, you'll need a top attorney."

"She's off-limits, I said."

"Why?"

"She's my daughter, Holden . . . but she doesn't know that."

"Give me a clearer picture," Holden said.

"That's clear enough."

"Then I'll say good-bye. The breakfast was grand. It's the first time I had an omelette with grapes."

"I had a fling with her mother," Phipps said. "The girl was born. I had no intention of marrying the woman. She sued. We settled out of court. It was a substantial sum."

"And you found a husband for her?"

"No. She did that on her own."

"And Gloria thinks the other guy is her dad?"

"Now you have it. Will you work for me or not?"

"I have a couple of problems. You're a little crazy and I'd prefer not to go to the slammer. But what the hell. I'll tag along . . . on two conditions. I want to be president of Aladdin Furs, the chief officer, with voting privileges."

"And what does that make me?"

"How should I know? Find yourself a title. Chairman of the board . . . you can be the main wizard."

"All right. Gloria will have to prepare the papers. And what else?"

"I want the exact location of where the district attorney is hiding my fiancée."

"You'll get it."

"When?" Holden asked.

"Soon."

"Then soon is when I start."

The old man smiled, and Holden didn't like the length of that grin.

Phipps removed a piece of paper from his cardigan and unfolded it for Sidney Holden, who discovered a single word.

Elsinore

"Elsinore? And no address? What is Elsinore?"

"A nursing home in Queens."

"Oh, he's a smart monkey, that Paul. He hides her . . . and she's ten minutes from his door. What if he finds out where I got this bit of news?"

"I could break Abruzzi before you finish your omelette."

"Then why the hell do you need me?"

"I told you," Phipps said. "I'm not getting into the life all alone."

"Forgive me if I'm nosy, but what are you going to find when you get there?"

"Fun," the old man said. "I have no appetite. I'm too old to be with women. Oh, the doctors could fix me up with some kind of clay prick. But the desire isn't there."

"So you'll go slumming. A life of crime. It's not as romantic as you think."

"I was a bootlegger once," Phipps said. "Believe me, it wasn't romantic. Then I moved molasses and tea. And when I was fifty-five, I started this foundation. Call it whatever you want, the robber baron makes good. But it was only one more empire, Holden, one more power link. The more people I helped, the surlier I got."

"So we go out on the road and make a little trouble."

"And business," Phipps said.

"Thank you . . . I'll be in touch."

"What does that mean?"

"I want to visit my fiancée."

"Holden, be here tomorrow at nine, or I swear, I'll have Abruzzi's own men chop you down."

Holden smiled. "That's not the way to treat your future companion."

And he parted company with the old man, left him with his cane and his rubber boots, and that ghost city he'd constructed for his own meals. Holden preferred a fish sandwich at Blimpie's or some ratatouille at home. And then he had to remind himself. His home was in that ceiling of stars downstairs in Phipps' lobby.

4

Elsinore wasn't hard to find. It was a country where a guy named Hamlet once lived. Holden had read the play in high school. He remembered poison going into somebody's ear. And a mad princess. A queen who liked to kiss her son on the mouth. A prince who went around killing people. Hamlet was a bumper, like Sidney Holden.

And this Elsinore was near the old Flushing airport. On a side street, in College Point. But Hamlet forgot to bring his sword. And Holden wasn't wearing his shooter this afternoon. He didn't have Hamlet's noblesse oblige. He couldn't afford to bump people at a nursing home. Elsinore was a great wooden hut with porches and a tin roof. There weren't any weirdos drifting out on the porch, or keepers in white suits. It could have been the oversized cottage of a shingle salesman in College Point. But there was one clue. The street was on a tiny hill, and Holden could see across Flushing Bay to the roofs of

Rikers Island. So he was in the mood for penitentiaries when he knocked on the nursing home's front door.

He expected a fuss. Shooflies with submachine guns. Nurses with clubs. Some poor old slob of an actor shouting Shakespeare. The usual hurly-burly of a mad-person's inn. But it was a tranquil place where Abruzzi had put his daughter-in-law. The waiting rooms sat above the sea. The water was dark and green, and Holden felt like some voyager on a route he hadn't charted for himself. Captain Sid.

He didn't have to go through a circle of secretaries. Holden got to the chief resident in a couple of minutes. And it disturbed him, because he liked the guy and he didn't want to. The resident was younger than Holden, and he didn't play the psychiatric genius. Dr. Herbert Garden.

"We were expecting you," the doctor said. "I've been told how persistent you can be."

"How come Paul doesn't have one of his shooters in the house?"

"I'd be an idiot, Mr. Holden, if I allowed detectives to run around scaring patients."

"But why did Paul pick this place? He must know lots of inns."

"Maybe he thought I could help Mrs. Abruzzi."

"She won't be Mrs. Abruzzi for long," Holden said. "I'm going to marry her when she's feeling better."

"How did you meet Mrs. Abruzzi?"

"Well, it's complicated," Holden said. "I rescued her from three friends of mine."

"I read about that incident in *Newsday*. But no rescuer was ever mentioned."

"Right. I'm not a sheriff, Dr. Garden. I don't wear a badge. I have to creep around the law. Big Paul was feuding with the Pinzolo brothers. Mike, Ed, and the Rat. They grabbed her, and I had to get her from Mike."

"And that's how you met."

"Well, I went out to Rockaway. That's where they were holding her. In a bungalow. I had a talk with Red Mike. And then Fay appeared, without her clothes. It was Mike's idea. They were holding her like that, so she couldn't run away. . . . I didn't have a choice. I loved Mikey and his brothers. I grew up with them, but Mikey wouldn't give her back."

"And who were you working for?"

"I can't disclose that."

"I'm sorry," Garden said. "I didn't mean to pry. But I have to examine the moment, the moment you met."

"She was naked. And I shot the three brothers."

"Did you wait until she left the room?"

"No. She saw me in the act."

"That's how it started then, Fay's decline. She must have felt guilty about their deaths, more than she could imagine. She fell in love with you, which made her their executioner. And how could she resolve that, Mr. Holden?"

"I'm not sure," Holden said. "By killing me, I suppose."

"And herself. She stopped making love. Wouldn't eat. Wouldn't talk. Isn't that how it was?"

"But will she get better, Doc?"

"Perhaps. But I don't think she'll ever be able to live with you again."

"Can I see her?"

"She won't recognize you," Garden said. "She can't afford to. Not now."

"But can I see her? For a second."

"Yes. Why not? But this is my ship, Holden. When I say jump, you jump. I don't want an argument. I don't want a fight."

"Agreed," Holden said, and he followed Dr. Garden across a narrow corridor. There didn't seem to be anyone aboard Garden's ship. Holden didn't meet a patient or a fucking nurse. Garden knocked on a door and said, "Darling, may I come in?"

Holden didn't like that word. Fay was *his* darling. But he didn't argue with the doctor.

Garden knocked again.

"Fay. It's Herbert. And a friend. We'd like to come in."

Garden entered, with Holden behind him. Fay's curly hair was gone. She had a boy's scalp. She wore a white hospital gown without a bra. Her eyes didn't have the slightest touch of fever, as if she'd been transported somewhere else, gone through some horrible looking glass.

"Hello, Herbert," she said. "How are you?"

"Fine, Fay. Would you like to meet my friend?"

"Oh, yes," she said with all the polite enthusiasm of the damned and the dead.

Holden's legs were shaking.

Garden introduced him. "This is Sidney Holden."

Fay took his hand. "It's kind of you to come."

He couldn't open his mouth.

"Would you care for a Perrier?"

"I think Sidney has to go, darling," the doctor said.

"It's a pity. We have so many things to talk about. . . . Make him promise that he'll come again."

"Oh, he's loyal," the doctor said. "He wouldn't leave you in the lurch."

And Holden ran outside to the toilet and threw up his breakfast into the sink. Holden looked up when he saw Garden in the mirror.

"I'm sorry you had to see her like that. But you insisted."

And Holden left Elsinore without rinsing his mouth.

He'd have gone to the Amazon, lived among whatever savages were around, but it wouldn't have cured Holden's disease. He'd never rescued Fay. He'd killed his friend Mike and brought her slowly to her doom. He didn't return to the Copenhagen to lick himself clean. He was like some forest animal who needed Mr. Phipps. But something bothered him about Phipps' little presentation in that giant breakfast room. Ninety-two-year-old man seeks adventure and hires Holden as his guide. Phipps' whole story began to stink.

And Holden visited the one encyclopedist he knew. Tosh, an eccentric book dealer who gathered information for bloodhounds and the mob. Tosh had his own morgue, like the *New York Times*. Six rooms of files. He'd never really been Holden's rat. Tosh was much too independent. Mob lawyers liked to use him because Tosh himself was an encyclopedia of crime. His files were open day and night, but Tosh was no bachelor, no night fish. He had a wife and three kids who lived in the rooms above his inventory, and he was a devoted husband and dad. Holden admired him for that. Tosh might have disappeared into all the paper and the dust without his family.

He'd had a year of Harvard, but Cambridge, Mass., must have been like the Sahara to Tosh. The bookworm needed New York. There was so much discipline in his head, so much on file, that he'd never have survived without the instant anarchy of the streets. He was handsome and tall, and sometimes he used Holden's tailor, even with all the dust on his sleeves.

"Tosh," Holden said, "you could have been an actor, another Gregory Peck."

They were sitting in Tosh's bookstore on Hudson Street.

"I used to be an actor," Tosh said.

"You never told me that."

"Yeah, I played the tree in *Waiting for Godot*. I swear to God. They needed a prop. I was the tree. And I got curtain calls, Holden. Audiences loved me. But I couldn't hack it, theater life. Late hours, slobbering over drama critics . . . How can I help?"

"This billionaire wants to hire me. Howard Phipps. Toshie, what do you have on him?"

"Off the cuff? He's not as rich as the Gettys or the Rothschilds."

"How did he make it?"

"He built up companies, one at a time. Took tiny outfits and managed them like a hawk."

"He swears he was a bootlegger."

"I don't think he ever legged."

"And his philanthropies?"

"They're legit. But I doubt if he loses money on them."

"The woman who runs his foundation, you have anything on her? The name is Vanderwelle."

"She must be new," Toshie said.

"Can you dig into her history . . . and the old man's?"

"Holden, I'm never sure what I have."

"I know that, Tosh. But I'll help you. He's ninety-two."

"Why don't you go upstairs and visit with the wife? Come back down in an hour."

And Holden went upstairs to sit with Mrs. Tosh. Why couldn't he fall in love with a sane woman? He'd picked Andrushka out of a showroom when she'd been selling herself to whatever buyers would have her. And he'd had to kill three men to find a path to Fay.

He returned to Toshie's downstairs office.

"His name isn't Phipps," Tosh said. "It's Feldstein."

"A Yid?"

"Without a doubt."

"Where was he born?"

"In Milwaukee," Tosh said. "And he's not ninety-two. He's eighty-nine."

"Who the hell would lie about a thing like that? He must have wanted my sympathy."

"Holden, I sell facts. Not motives."

And suddenly Holden was more interested in Howard Feldstein Phipps than he'd ever been in a man.

"A Yid, you say."

"And also a bit of a rabbi."

"I'm speechless," Holden said. "A rabbi? Where did he practice?"

"Holden, he didn't have a congregation, or anything like that. He studied at a cantor's college."

"What's that?"

"You know, a cantor. Sings all the holy songs. Leads the choir. He was a terrific grosser."

"I don't understand."

"A cantor with a good voice was like an opera star. Had an agent and everything . . . Holden, he was a hired gun. Went from synagogue to synagogue. All over the country. You had to book him a year in advance."

"When was this?"

"Around nineteen twenty-two."

"But he was a child. Nineteen or twenty."

"That's not so young for a cantor," Toshie said. "But something happened. He fucked up in Chicago. There was a scandal. The big synagogues wouldn't hire him. And guess what? He shows up in Seattle as a Pinkerton man."

Toshie started to laugh, but Holden couldn't get out of his gloom.

"Don't you think it's funny? From cantor's college to the Pinkertons. That's when he became Phipps. He leaves the agency in 'twenty-nine, and bingo, it all starts for him. He buys, he sells, with terrific concentration. The country goes into a depression, and Phipps becomes a billionaire."

"What about the girl? Gloria Vanderwelle."

"Holden, I didn't come up with a thing."

"All right. What do we have? He's a Yid. He sings for a living. He stops. He's a Pinkerton. Then he makes his first million. . . . Now he's eighty-nine, he grows bored, and hires Sidney Holden. He talks about funny paper, and he wants to hit the road. Why?"

"He's in trouble," Tosh said. "There's a saboteur in his operation. Maybe more than one. His companies are tumbling, two at a time. His accounts are running dry."

"So it's a crisis. He can hire whoever he wants. Some big law firm with a whole team of bloodhounds. They'd find the leaks, wouldn't they? Why me?"

"I don't have the facts," Toshie said.

"Why me? I'm retired, Tosh. You know that."

"But the cantor doesn't."

5

Holden was at Phipps' cathedral restaurant a minute before nine.

He couldn't bear to look at the food the waiters brought. He drank a cup of hot water, with a lemon slice, while the old man had a dish of breakfast curry.

"Lost your appetite, Sid?"

"Well, I saw my fiancée. She didn't recognize me."

"I'm sorry, but you ought to eat. We're going on a long trip . . . to Chappy."

"Never heard of the place."

"Chappaquiddick. To collect some funny paper."

"Just like that?"

"It's been arranged, Holden. We leave in half an hour."

"I never travel without twenty-four hours' notice."

"You'll have to break your rules. It can't be helped. The money is waiting for us in Chappaquiddick."

"Let it wait."

The old man began to diminish in front of Sidney

Holden. The cardigan sat like an envelope around a bag of bones. "I can't go by myself. . . ."

"You could raise an army in five minutes."

"Don't want an army. I want you."

"All right," Holden said.

And the bag of bones was gone. "Do you have a gun?"

"Yes. But it's at home."

"Then we'll have to collect it, won't we? Finish your breakfast, Mr. Holden."

Holden gulped the hot water. "Cheers."

They went down to Phipps' office to meet Mrs. Vanderwelle. She'd packed an overnight bag for the old man. And Sidney Holden had that same dilemma. He could sense the lines of her body under the suit she wore. The mouth was soft. But was she pretty, and why should he have cared? Holden wasn't looking to replace his darling. It didn't matter how damaged Fay was. He was devoted to her, even if she couldn't remember his name. He'd have to visit Elsinore again, bring her some roses, talk about Red Mike . . . with Dr. Garden.

He must have been inside a trance. Mrs. Vanderwelle tugged at him. "Some pocket money," she said. "For the trip."

She gave Holden a thick packet of twenty-dollar bills. He wanted to question her, but not in front of the old man.

"You'll take care of him, won't you? He mustn't forget to put on his pajamas."

And Holden started to dig. "Why don't you come along?"

"I wish I could. But I have the foundation . . . and Howard didn't invite me."

"I'll invite you," Holden said.

"Another time." And Holden understood now why it was so hard to make up his mind about Mrs. Vanderwelle. He couldn't meet her eyes. Under the tinted glasses, her eyes weren't there. She might have been looking at the wall while she chatted with Holden. It infuriated him. He was feeling homicidal, but he'd never have touched the lady.

He went down into the street with the old man, whose chauffeur appeared in a rented Plymouth. Holden could have found a better car in the meanest body shop. But Phipps wanted to be anonymous on the road to Chappaquiddick.

And while Holden had been measuring the Plymouth, the chauffeur disappeared.

"Who's going to drive us to Chappaquiddick?"

"You are."

"That's the limit," Holden said. "My dad was a chauffeur. I watched him suffer behind the wheel. It broke him, Mr. Phipps. It kept him a fucking child. I swore to myself that I'd never follow my dad into that line of work."

"But I can't take my chauffeur. It would ruin it for us. He'd know all our plans. . . . Get in. I'll drive."

"You're too old. And you have bad feet. I'll drive. But don't make it a habit. I'd have to quit."

"I'll sit up front with you, Sid. We're companions. I won't let you down."

He couldn't escape that shadow, the shadow of his dad. It was a recurrent dream, a nightmare Holden had endured since he could remember. Holden wearing some kind of livery while he sat behind the wheel.

Sidney Holden, the prince of chauffeurs in a peaked cap. But his uniform had eagles and stars and buttons of the United States. It was a soldier's livery. Holden's dad had been a soldier during the big war. But Holden couldn't tell who he was driving in all the dreams. Now he saw the face. It was God, God in the back seat, wearing the cardigan of Howard Phipps, that hidden singer of holy songs. And Holden had to laugh. God had been a Pinkerton man.

※

Phipps wanted to stop in New Haven for lunch. Holden shivered when he saw the towers of Yale. It was like coming to a foreign country, and he panicked for a moment, thinking they'd need some currency with a queen's head. Oh, he'd dealt with Yalies before. He'd even been to the Yale Club in Manhattan. But the college startled him. He expected to see monks riding around on bicycles, and all he met were kids and tweedy men, dressed like they were living in a kind of noble poverty, a knighthood of books and baggy pants. Holden was glad he'd gone to Bernard Baruch.

Phipps led him to a neighborhood behind the college. There were no towers. The streets were broken, and black children played in the rubble. Holden couldn't find a restaurant. There was a merciless regularity to the small, dark buildings, like the inner walls of a heartland Holden had never heard about. The town was like Phipps himself, porous, with a lot of different pasts.

And then, in those dark streets, Holden discovered a tiny Italian restaurant that didn't have a signboard or a name in the window. Holden parked in front of the restaurant, and the two of them went inside and sat down. The waiters ignored them until Phipps shouted in some Italian dialect that must have been born in the streets of New Haven, because suddenly the waiters danced. A tablecloth materialized, together with silver, and a blue candle that no one would let Holden light all by himself.

"What did you say, Mr. Phipps?"

"I told them that their mothers slept with strangers, and their fathers only fucked cows and sheep, and if they didn't serve us in a second, you would piss on the wall and fuck their baby sisters."

"They could have gotten angry, and I would have had to fight the whole restaurant."

"Holden, you're wrong. They love to be cursed. That's the language that's dear to them."

"When was the last time you ate in this restaurant?"

"Twenty years ago."

"Then why were you so sure the same trick would work?"

"I took a chance. I've always been a gambler."

Holden's nausea was gone. He had a bowl of tortellini soup, with great hunks of bread. Black wine arrived in tiny glasses. Holden drank six. He had chicken and potatoes. Broccoli and carrots. He had chocolate cake.

"You're a glutton," the old man said. "I couldn't afford to keep you, Sid. You'd bankrupt me with an appetite like that. Want another dessert?"

He whistled to the waiter in that special Italian of his, and they brought Holden a wedge of cake with towers and canopies of hazelnuts and dark cream. Holden took a bite, and he would have killed for that piece of cake. "What's it called?"

"In English, Sid? College pie. It's a local dish."

They had cups of coffee to wake Holden from the black wine. Then they got up and shook hands with all the waiters. But Holden never saw the bill.

"How come they didn't charge us?" he asked in the street.

"It would take an hour to answer."

"I have the time."

"This was one of my hunting grounds a long time ago. They recognized that from the way I spoke. They wouldn't have dared charge us for the meal."

"And what did you hunt in New Haven?"

"Whales. The hooch we delivered was kept in big white barrels called whales."

"Ah, when you were a bootlegger," Holden said. "Did you bless the barrels with kosher songs?"

The old man fixed his bumper's eyes on Holden. "What kosher songs?"

"Don't take it to heart. A friend of mine says you were a cantor once."

"Do I look like a cantor?"

"I wouldn't know."

"Have you been investigating me, Sid? What did you find?"

"Very little. You were born in Milwaukee. You went to cantor's college. You were a big draw in the best synagogues, but you had to pull out. You surfaced again as a Pinkerton man in Seattle. And your name is Feldstein, not Phipps."

"Your friend has an active imagination," Phipps said. "I could show you my birth certificate."

"Mr. Phipps, should I tell you how many birth certificates I keep in my drawer? I have enough social security numbers to field a baseball team. There were times when I had to disappear too. My dad loved the New York Giants. So I'm Johnny Mize. Jack Lohrke. Mel Ott."

"And I'm Howard Phipps."

They drove to Woods Hole and sat in a line of cars near the ferry slip. There was a fog over the water, and the ferry arrived out of the gloom. Holden heard the engines, and the boat docked with a soft bump. The ferry door opened and cars drove out of the ferry's big barn. Holden stared into that ribbed well and thought of a whale's mouth. Phipps shouldn't have mentioned whales.

Then it was Holden's turn to drive into the barn. He didn't want to sit in that enormous well. "Shouldn't we go up to the deck? We don't have to be baby-sitters for a goddamn car."

"It's safer here," Phipps said.

"I don't get it."

"It's safer here. You can never tell who we might meet up on the deck. It takes one push, Sid, and we're overboard."

"Is somebody after you, Mr. Phipps?"

"Not at all. But we'll be carrying a lot of paper on the return trip. And it's better for both of us if we're not conspicuous. . . . Stay in the car."

And so they sat inside the whale. The ocean beat against the metal door with a thick boom that sent tiny shivers through the ferry. It felt like some sort of attack, that relentless drive of water. The ferry leaked. Water spilled in through the bottom of the door and a pool began to build under the stairs to the main deck.

"We could drown," Holden said.

"I've been on this ferry a hundred times, and no one ever drowned."

The engines stopped, and Holden heard that same bump of metal against wood. The door lowered like a drawbridge and the cars bumped over the door and onto Martha's Vineyard.

They drove to Edgartown and waited for another ferry. They had to cross the channel to Chappaquiddick. It was too far to spit across, and Holden could tell that the current was mean. The ferry had no doors. It was an open green box, and Holden watched the ferryman at his wheel.

It took half a minute to get across the creek.

Holden couldn't find a village on Chappy.

Sand and trees and a country club, houses with gray shingles, a couple of barns. It was his idea of what an island ought to be, a home for lots of Robinson Crusoes.

They stopped at a junkyard that reached across several fields. Holden saw stoves from the time of Martha Washington, toilet commodes, the bottom of a ferry, weather vanes, rotting wood and rust. Entire fields had that bright orange look of decay.

A pack of dogs guarded the junk. They weren't wild. They were meant to growl at strangers. The dogs surrounded the car and slobbered the windows with their wet jaws.

"It's time to get out," Phipps said.

"With those dogs? They're attackers, Mr. Phipps."

Phipps got out of the car, whacked the nearest dog with his cane, and the other dogs scampered to the next rusty field.

"Leave the key. No one steals on Chappy."

They ventured into that rust.

The dogs grew courageous and barked at Holden, but only from a distance.

There was a house behind the junkyard, with the same orange color. The old man whistled once. The sound shot across the fields and rang in Holden's ear. Then a whistling came from the house. It was like birds calling, the birds of Chappaquiddick.

They entered the house. Three old men sat behind a table. It was a family, a father and his two sons. The sons had to be seventy-five, and the father could have been a hundred. Phipps introduced them as the Coleridges. Ethan and his sons, Minot and Paul. Holden smiled at all the aliases. The Coleridges were the Cardinales, gunmen who ran Providence for fifty years until federal attorneys chased them out of the rackets. All three were wanted for murder. Holden couldn't imagine a hundred-year-old man sitting on his ass in the pen.

"This is the baron of Rhode Island," Phipps said, touching Ethan's shoulder.

"Phippsy, you shouldn't exaggerate. Why brag to the boy?"

"Because he's one of us. Sidney Holden."

"Never heard of him," Ethan Coleridge said.

"Don't you read the papers?"

"Was he in the *Vineyard Gazette?*" Minot asked, and fumbled with his hearing aid.

"That's a stupid question," Phipps said. "He's not a local."

"Phippsy, don't rile my boy."

"But that's the problem," Phipps said. "You're stuck here on Chappy, and you don't get the news."

"Chappy's fine. You ought to come and live with us . . . you and the boy. There's nothing on the other side of the creek, nothing that's worth cooing about."

"Come on. You can't even get cable TV."

"We're happy. I play checkers with my boys. We have the run of the land. The rest of the world is one big graveyard."

"I agree with my dad," Paul said, and this was the brother who worried Holden. The quiet ones were always the first to go mad.

"Phippsy, ask the boy what he thinks," Ethan said.

"I agree and disagree," Holden said. "I like your island, Mr. Coleridge. I really do. I could live here. But I'd be unhappy about the thought of never seeing London again."

"London?" Ethan said. "A pigsty."

"Have you ever been?" Holden asked.

"Have I been to London? No. But there's nothing to miss."

"The best sandwiches I ever had came from Holland Park. And there's nothing like tea at Brown's. You have to reserve a chair for high tea."

"Dad," Minot said. "Make him stop."

"Don't be rude to the boy," Ethan said.

"I mean, he's talking like one of those cosmopolites. We don't ride on planes. And we don't drink tea. I play checkers with my dad and I win . . . dada, he's wearing a gun. It's bulging out of his pants."

"What do you expect him to wear? He's Phippsy's agent."

"But he could have left it on the porch."

"We're friends, Minot, don't you forget that."

"Give them the paper, dad, and tell them to blow."

"I can't do that, son. Phippsy was my protégé. He gave you presents when you were a toddler. He gave you toys."

"I don't like his friend," Paul said.

And Holden blamed himself for becoming Phipps' companion. Now he'd have to strangle a seventy-five-year-old man.

"Ah, I know how you feel," Phipps said. "Strangers upset them. They were always shy, your boys. . . ."

"They're like animals," Ethan said. "They never married . . . and after their mama died, they couldn't stand another woman in the house. I wanted to marry again. You know what Paul said? 'We'll kill you and the whore, dad.' I'm their prisoner, Phippsy, swear to God."

"Who'd ever marry you, dad?" Minot said. "You can't pee straight any more. And you have a tube in your dick."

"Brother," Paul said, "why are you telling this to strangers, giving them intimate details about our father?"

"You're right," Minot said. "Give them the money, will you?"

The brothers smiled, and Ethan started to shake.

"Boys, I want no violence in this house."

"Violence, dad?" Minot said. "We're giving them their cash. . . . Fetch it, brother."

Paul went into a back room and returned with a pair of enormous suitcases. The leather had that same maddening orange rust. Minot must have salvaged them from the junkyard.

Holden picked up the suitcases; his eyes began to water from all that weight.

"Good-bye, Ethan," Phipps said. "Good-bye, Minot. Good-bye, Paul." He hugged the baron of Rhode Island and tried to hug Minot and Paul, but the boys moved away from him and smiled.

"Count the paper," Minot said.

"I trust you. I know your father almost seventy years. I worked for him, Minot."

"Count the paper."

Phipps turned to Holden. "Please."

Holden unbuckled the first suitcase. It was stuffed with a potpourri: packages of fives, tens, twenties, and thousand-dollar bills. Holden had never seen a thousand-dollar bill before. He felt like some king of the currency. But the king was more like a fool, counting on his knees. He unbuckled the second suitcase. No one talked. Ethan looked like a sick snake. It took Holden half an hour to count all the cash. He buckled up the suitcases and carried three million two hundred twenty thousand and sixty dollars to the door.

"See you, sonny," Minot said.

Holden began to grumble once he left the house with Phipps. "How am I going to carry this, Phippsy, across three fucking fields?" The sun had gone down and Holden knew the dogs were out there.

"Stay," Phipps said. "I'll fetch the car."

"No."

"Then let me carry one of the cases."

"No. I don't like your friends, Phippsy. They belong in an institution."

"Ah, Ethan's all right. And the boys are bitter. You heard Ethan. They never married."

"What kind of deal did you make?"

"It wasn't a deal. The money's mine. I came to collect it, that's all."

And Holden trudged across the fields of junk with Phipps behind him. He had to stop and rest after fifty feet. His hands were torn by the time they reached the car. None of the dogs had bothered them.

Holden put the suitcases in the trunk. Then he drove toward the ferry.

"Phippsy, you might have had an agreement with the father, but not with the sons. We'll be lucky to get off the Vineyard alive."

"They wouldn't go against their father," Phipps said.

"They're bumpers," Holden said. "And they're crazy."

The ferryman took them across the creek, and already Holden was suspicious. He didn't like the ferryman's dumb smile.

"We'll stay on the island tonight," Phipps said. "I booked a room in Edgartown."

"I don't think that's such a hot idea. We ought to distance ourselves from those boys."

"We're staying at the Charlotte Inn."

They drove to South Summer Street and Holden parked in a little lot. He carried the suitcases into the inn. Phipps signed the book. And then Holden managed to get the money up the stairs to their room. He wasn't so jumpy inside the Charlotte Inn. The furniture and the little crooked hallways reminded him of Brown's, where Holden liked to stop in London, when he was stealing patterns for his tailor. He loved the wallpaper at Brown's, the adventures he had exploring the hotel, finding a corner where he could sit and read a book. There were always clergymen around, factory owners from Devon or Lancashire, and Yanks like himself. But he could never understand English hotels, because no one hounded him for the bill. The idea of cash seemed beneath the dignity of a hotel. And Holden had the illusion of staying at Brown's for free.

And so the Charlotte Inn soothed him, and he didn't worry so much about Ethan's boys. He had his shooter. He could relax a bit. And somehow he didn't believe that they would wander into the inn and start knocking on doors in the middle of the night. But they weren't rational beings. They'd been hiding too long, living with their dad, and Holden didn't take a chance. He slept with the gun.

The room had a fireplace and a soft couch and an old clock that ticked in Holden's ear. He built a fire for the old man, crumpling paper around the logs. Holden missed his VCR. It felt like a good night for *The Big Sleep*. He opened one of the suitcases and borrowed a thousand-dollar bill.

The old man had gone into the toilet and sat for an hour. Then Holden began to hear a rabbity noise, like a small animal crying. "Phippsy," he said through the door. "Are you in trouble?"

Phipps didn't answer at first. Then he said, "Come in, please."

But the toilet was locked.

"Open up."

"I can't."

And Holden had to stab at the lock with his pocket-knife. It took him another five minutes to enter the toilet. The old man was sitting on the pot with his pajama bottoms caught between his legs.

"I'm a bloody invalid. I need a nurse."

"It's nothing," Holden said, untangling the old man.

And they went to sleep in their twin beds, Holden with his gun, his mind like a night crawler, picking at sounds while he dreamt. The old man snored.

𝒩

They had breakfast downstairs in an enclosed garden. Fresh orange juice and English muffins and cups of coffee with cream. There was a great clutter outside the inn. A film crew had captured Edgartown. Holden saw caravans and trailers and lighting trucks. Men with walkie-talkies stood on the trucks and breathed signals across the town. They were shooting *Jaws* 5. And Holden wondered what kind of shark they'd concocted for the film.

"Sid," the old man said, "did you ever think of changing careers? You dress like an actor. Where'd you learn to walk without a wrinkle?"

"It's not the walk," Holden said. "It's the quality of the wool." And he carried the suitcases down to the car. But Phipps didn't want them buried in the trunk.

"The back seat will do."

They caught the noon ferry. Holden sat with Phipps in the car barn. The engines churned, and water began to spill into the barn. The same puddles formed. Holden thought the car would float off in a lake inside the barn. Phipps wasn't worried about water. He watched the suitcases. And that was fatal. Because he didn't see Minot and Paul standing outside the car in their galoshes, holding Webley automatics with very long noses. And when Holden saw them, it was already too late. The boys had come from his blind side. They tapped on the window with their Webleys. The last time Holden had seen such long guns was in a British spy film, with Peter Lorre. He almost started to laugh.

"Open," Minot said.

"They can screw," Phipps said.

"Phippsy," Holden said. "We're not immortal. They can poke us right through the glass."

He opened his door. Minot reached in. "You're naive, grandpa. Did you really think you'd get off the island with our stash?"

"It's my paper," Phipps said.

"But you shouldn't have let us sit on it so long."

Paul opened the rear door and collected both suitcases. Holden still couldn't understand the old boy's agility. He carried the suitcases across that little lake, up the stairs, and out of the barn.

Minot smiled. "I think I'll sit and watch the scenery with you, if you don't mind. I promised dad I wouldn't hurt a hair off your head, Mr. Phipps, unless I had to. He cried when I told him about this journey we were taking. 'Phippsy's my oldest friend.'"

Minot must have been an actor in public school. He

was much too involved with his own narration. He gestured with the Webley, and Holden picked it right out of his hand. And when he struggled to get his gun back, Holden dug the silencer into the old boy's mouth.

"Here, Phipps, take the gun. And if he blinks, blow his brains out. We have nothing to lose."

And Holden had to go up those stairs to look for Paul. He wandered into that little lake wearing three-hundred-dollar shoes. His socks had come from the Duke of Windsor's closets. He went all around the ferry, from deck to deck. The ocean looked like coiling skin. He searched under the lifeboats, in the ferry's luncheonette, in the storage bins. He wondered if Paul could have vanished inside the pilot room. Then he turned the corner and found Paul sitting on the suitcases and eating a hot dog. Paul was so busy with his dog, he never looked up. Wasn't a soul around. Holden could have tossed him into the Atlantic, but he was done with all that.

His instincts had gone bad. He'd forgotten that Paul had bumped before Holden was born. The old boy had sniffed Holden's shadow. He reached for his Webley, and Holden hit him twice in the throat. Paul's eyes bulged. Then he fell into Holden's arms. Holden took the Webley and tossed it over the rail. The gun arced out, started to spin, and dropped like a hammer into the sea.

Suddenly Holden had fingers at his throat. He'd hit the old boy as hard as he could, but it wasn't hard enough. Their eyes locked, and Holden understood what a career Paul must have had. Ten years ago Sidney Holden wouldn't have had a chance. There was no pity in Paul's eyes, no alarm. He wasn't burdened with memories of Cézanne or a fiancée who'd lost her reason. And he didn't have Andrushka's long legs to think about. Just murder and money. Paul found Holden's windpipe, but not fast enough. He could have suffered from arthritis. Holden slapped Paul's elbows apart, then hit him again. He had to leave the suitcases for a moment. Three million plus riding above the spray. He sat Paul down in a deck chair and hooked him to the chair with Paul's old belt. It was a trick he'd learnt from a bumper in the fur market. Paul would sit like that until he woke.

He discovered two linen handkerchiefs in the old boy's pockets, wrapped them around his own hands, and carried the suitcases down to the car. Minot still sat with the gun in his mouth.

"Phippsy, let him go."

"You're crazy."

"He can't hurt us. Let him go."

The ferry was about to dock.

"You don't give the orders," Phipps said.

Holden took the gun out of Minot's mouth.

"Minot, you're too fucking old for this."

"Where's my brother?"

"Taking a little sun. Get out of the car."

Minot got out. He stood there like a lost child while Holden drove out of the barn.

The Pinkerton Man

6

Holden went out to Elsinore.

Dr. Garden wasn't there.

Garden's sanitarium had one attendant, a fat man who wasn't unfriendly. He wore a guard's uniform with a dress tie. He didn't have a nightstick or a gun. He had a pencil holder clipped to his pants.

"I'd like to see my fiancée."

"I wish I could help you," the guard said. "But I can't."

"Where is everybody?"

"Out on a picnic."

"When will they be back?"

"The doctor has his own bus. He drives them to a lot of places."

"He took the whole caboodle? Nurses and . . ."

"It ain't a regular nuthouse. He don't do shock therapy and all that shit. He tells his patients to swim."

"Where's the pool?" Holden asked.

"It's somewhere, but I've never seen it."

The guard didn't prevent him from wandering through

Elsinore. Holden went into Garden's office. The furniture was gone. There wasn't a diploma on the wall, not a single scroll that would suggest an institution, not a stitch of paper with the word "Elsinore" on it.

He returned to the guard.

"You never met Dr. Garden."

"No."

"Who hired you?"

"I'm not sure."

"That's convenient," Holden said. "You work for an agency?"

"It's my own getup. I'm an actor, currently unemployed."

"And you just wandered into this gig, huh?"

"A woman called me. Left three hundred dollars in my mailbox. She gave me the address and told me to sit."

"For how long?"

"Didn't say."

"Did she tell you I would come?"

"Yeah. You're Sidney Holden. But she said you wouldn't hurt me if I was nice."

"What did she sound like, this woman on the phone? Young? Old?"

"Young," the guard said.

"Cultured?"

"I couldn't tell."

"What's your name?"

"Lavender Hall."

"No one's named Lavender Hall," Holden said.

"That's my stage name . . . Lavender Hall."

"Give me your wallet."

"Why?"

"Your wallet."

The fat man had a driver's license, a social security number, and a swimming pass under the name of Lavender Hall.

"All right. I believe you. . . . That woman calls again, you get in touch with me, understand? Night or day, you call."

Holden scribbled his name and number on the back of Lavender Hall's swimming pass and handed him two hundred dollars.

"You're in my stable now."

"I don't get you," the fat man said.

"Sonny, you belong to me."

Holden's natural juices had come back. He was gathering spies again. He could provide the lightning for a lot of storms. He went to his encyclopedist, Tosh. He handed Toshie the thousand-dollar bill he'd swiped from Phipps.

"Holden, are you collecting antiques? This bill is older than you."

"But is it for real?" Holden said.

"Of course it's for real. Only an imbecile would queer a thousand-dollar bill. You can't pass off that kind of denomination. You'd have the whole Treasury department after your ass."

"I figured as much. But check it for me. There's always that odd chance . . ."

They moved to the back of Toshie's bookshop. Tosh laid the bill inside a machine that looked like a pants presser with a window on top. He locked that pants presser and Grover Cleveland's face appeared in the window, big as Tosh. The image startled Holden. He could see all the dots and dashes around Grover Cleveland's neck, all the flurry of lines, the simple cross-hatching of any thousand-dollar bill. But that old fat president still haunted Holden.

"Watch the eyes, Holden. Watch the eyes."

"I'm watching."

"No counterfeiter could imitate that look. The eyes stare right out at you."

"Toshie, I'm getting the creeps. The face is fucking alive."

Tosh laughed and unlocked the pants presser. "Who told you the bill was bad? That cantor, Phipps?"

"Yeah. He says he wasn't a cantor."

"He's full of crap."

"What about his daughter, Tosh? Mrs. Vanderwelle."

"There is no Mrs. Vanderwelle."

"If her name isn't Vanderwelle, what is it?"

"Church."

"That's the name of Phipps' old sweetheart. I remember. Judith Church."

"This one is also Judith."

"A pair of Judiths? So why does little Judith call herself Gloria Vanderwelle?"

"Beats the shit out of me," Tosh said.

"What does big Judith do for a living?"

"She doesn't have to do much. Phipps supports her. But she's a drama coach on the side. And she has her own little theater company, the Manhattan Mimes. They do a lot of pantomime and straight stuff."

"How'd you learn so much about the lady?"

"I told you. I was an actor once. I even studied with Judith for a while."

"Did you ever meet little Judith?"

"I don't think so," Toshie said.

"What's you theory? Mine is that mother and daughter might be bleeding the old man. So he has to come up with cash to stuff all the leaks."

"I don't speculate, Holden. I'm your facts man. But I wouldn't mess with those two girls. If they have the cantor on a string, imagine what they could do to you."

"I'll be careful, Tosh."

Holden had Phipps and the two Judiths on his agenda, but he stopped off at the Algonquin to find Paul Abruzzi. The district attorney liked to hold court in the lounge. It had become his throne room. He was sitting with several Democratic precinct captains when Holden arrived, men with black teeth who gathered votes for Paul in the outlands of Edgemere and Hollis. Paul was always conspiring with political captains. He ran the borough of Queens from his table at the Algonquin. Paul dismissed the captains when he saw Sidney Holden.

"How are you, son?"

"I'm in love with Fay."

"That's your misfortune," the district attorney said. "Did you come out of your latest rathole to tell me that? I don't want trouble, Sidney. I hear you've been running with Howard Phipps."

"Does that scare you, Paul?"

"Yes it does. The man can do me a lot of harm."

"Who kidnapped Fay from Elsinore?"

"I don't know what you're talking about."

"Elsinore. You put her in that nursing home in College Point."

"She never went near College Point. You don't have

all your marbles, Sidney. I could get you a psychiatrist."

"I saw Fay's psychiatrist. And I saw Fay. At Elsinore."

"You've been having too many wet dreams."

"Where is she then?"

"Where she belongs. Away from you."

"Should I tell that to Howard Phipps?"

Paul's eyes shrank into his head. Holden understood that dark white mask. Paul was planning Holden's destruction. "Don't play that card, Sidney, or we'll all get hurt."

"Then listen to me, Paul. Somebody put Fay in Elsinore and somebody took her out. Check on it."

"I don't have to check. You're a public nuisance, son. Phipps will wake up to you, and when he does, it'll be all over. Now get the fuck out of here."

"Just tell me how she is."

"Holden."

"I won't bother you, Paul. Just tell me how she is."

"Holden."

"I'm not leaving. I don't care if the Algonquin has a house detective. Let him come for me. I don't care.

That white mask grew darker still. "She doesn't even remember you're alive. You're a zero to her, Holden, an absolute zero."

Holden's eyes twitched under the Algonquin's lights. He could have broken the district attorney's neck, but it wouldn't have gotten him nearer to Fay. Paul didn't seem to have the answers to Holden's riddles. Elsinore.

He went downtown to Aladdin Furs. The whole market was sensitive to Sidney Holden. He was more than a retired bumper, or a man whose face was inside *Vanity Fair*. He was the master of his own company, president of Aladdin. He didn't even know where his accountant was. His cutters and nailers were attending to the skins. His designer, Nick Tiel, was out of his skull, and Holden assumed the men worked from Nick's old patterns, because Nick had nothing new. Holden never asked. What was a president, after all? He didn't run the shop. And so far he hadn't even signed a check. Who would pay Holden if Holden couldn't pay himself?

He sat in his office, pondering his own presidency, when Phipps appeared in his favorite cardigan with Mrs. Vanderwelle, little Judith Church.

"You're a hard man to find," Phipps said. "I've been calling for days. Aren't you gonna invite us to sit down?"

"Not until you tell me who signs the checks for this establishment."

"Whoever you like, Sid. Take it up with Gloria."

"I'm sorry," Mrs. Vanderwelle said. "The new checks are at the printers."

"New checks?"

"Yes. With your name on the cover."

"But I don't know what each of my men makes."

"I'll give you a salary schedule once the checks arrive."

"And what about me?" Holden asked.

"Don't lay that on us," Phipps said. "You're the boss."

"But I haven't seen the books," Holden said. "What can we afford?"

"Whatever you're worth. Now can we sit?"

The old man and his secret daughter sat on the bed in Sidney Holden's office. "You're supposed to be my companion. I can't talk to you, Sid. You seem preoccupied."

"It's my fiancée. The district attorney stole her again."

"Can't you manage to keep your own fiancée?"

"I don't have badges and Detective Specials. I can't go to a judge and get some writ. All I have is my reputation."

"And your salary, don't forget. . . . All right. Where is big Paul?"

"At the Algonquin," Holden said.

"Dial the hotel, will you, dear?" Phipps asked Mrs. Vanderwelle.

She got the Algonquin on the line and handed the phone to Phipps.

"Paul Abruzzi, please. . . . Paul? Howard Phipps here. My man Holden seems to think you've been shuffling his fiancée around to a lot of different places. . . . Ah, I see. But Sid must have had some arrangement with her. I mean, he didn't invent the fact that she was living with him. . . . Thank you, Paul. I appreciate it."

Phipps returned the telephone to its cradle. "Your fiancée's at home. You shouldn't get involved with a married woman."

"When can I visit?"

"Soon as you like. The door's open to you, Sid."

Should he bring flowers or a potful of ratatouille from an East Side restaurant? He was helpless and half crazy. He wondered if he should wear another suit. He would have showered at his office if Phipps hadn't been there with little Judith. He would have found the right cologne. But what cologne was right for the occasion? He arrived with his tail between his legs, like some forlorn commando.

He rang Fay's bell. It was worse than fear, this loving Fay. Paul opened the door.

"You shouldn't have gone to Phipps."

"I didn't have much of a choice," Holden said. "I'm not the district attorney. Are you letting me in?"

"Of course. You're our hallowed guest. You bought Aladdin, I heard."

"It was a gift from the old man."

"Better still. You're the golden boy. Come, I'll bring you to Fay."

The blood beat brutally under Holden's eyes, as if he had a long spear in his cheek. She was just like that woman he'd met in Elsinore. But she wore a dress, not a white gown. He couldn't get used to Fay without her curls. She sat in a room with little gates on the windows. Paul had decided to bring his own Elsinore into the house. Holden didn't see any signs of the children or that playwright Rex. His darling was alone with Paul.

"Where's Rex and the kids?"

"On vacation," Paul said.

"Who takes care of her?"

"Nurses. But it's none of your business."

"And you stole her back from Elsinore."

"She's never been out of the apartment. Isn't that right, Fay?"

His darling nodded her head.

"And who is this man?"

Her lips moved, but she said nothing.

"Isn't he the Frog?"

"Frog," she said like a mechanical girl.

Holden was born in Avignon. He'd come here as a little boy, the son of an American soldier. He couldn't really remember who his mother had been. He was a "love child," a little frog who'd grown up in Queens.

"Would you like to go with the Frog? He wants to take you to Central Park West. He has his own tower."

Furrows appeared in her head, dark lines, like some horrible static. "I can't leave, Paul. I have my sewing lessons." She held out her hand. "Good-bye, Mr. Frog."

The prosecutor accompanied Holden to the door.

"You win, Paul."

"I didn't win, damn you. She's lost to us. And don't give me any more crap about that dumb nuthouse. Elsinore doesn't exist."

"She's not lost," Holden said. "She's gone into her own closet and she can't come out."

Holden walked away from Paul.

The prosecutor had to laugh. He'd defeated the wild boy, Sid Holden. Fay wouldn't run to any more towers on Central Park West. She'd become a baby, but so what? Holden couldn't have her. Paul had nurses around the clock to clean her potty chair. The same nurses had been teaching her how to knit and sew. The needles she had were as blunt as a Popsicle stick. The yarn was like wet paper. She'd been working on a pair of mittens for a month.

The phone rang. Fay's ears didn't even twitch to the sound of the bell. She was in a universe where telephones didn't matter. "Mr. Frog," she muttered.

Paul answered the phone on the sixth or seventh ring. "Abruzzi here. . . . Yes, boss. Holden was a lamb."

He got off the phone and started shouting for the

nurse. "Miranda, will you come, please? I think Fay has to go to the toilet. Jesus, she's all wet."

Miranda arrived. A tall black woman with purple lip ice. She reminded Paul of Holden's black "mama," Mrs. Howard. She moved like a sexy serpent. Paul couldn't take his mind off Miranda. He grieved for Fay, still loved her, in spite of her soiled clothes and vacant stares, but Paul was in the final bloom of his life. Soon he'd have his seat on the high court. The pols had promised it to him, and he would need a mistress like Miranda, who wouldn't have to give up her title as nurse of his entourage.

Miranda bent over Fay, and Paul could see the outline of her underpants. "Honey," she said, "we'll just take a little trip to the toilet. We'll get into the shower and I'll sing you a song."

"What kind of song?" Fay asked.

"Anything you like."

Paul's face was blue with desire. Miranda waltzed around him. Fay started to hum. "Froggy," she said.

And all the desire seemed to retreat from Paul. He'd have to kill Sid Holden one of these days.

7

Alone, without his darling, Frog sought out Judith Church and her Manhattan Mimes. The Mimes occupied a loft on Amsterdam, a few blocks north of Holden's tower. It took him three days to get an appointment with big Judith. He couldn't afford to look like the Duke of Windsor and expect to get close to the Mimes. And so he put on one of the outfits he would wear when he was in the habit of killing people. And he arrived at Judith's loft.

Now he understood Phipps. The babe had to be touching seventy, but she was almost as beautiful as Mrs. Howard, who'd lived with Holden's dad. Judith Church was the handsomest white woman Sidney Holden had ever seen. She didn't have any starch around the eyes, no rouge to obscure the wrinkled skin. Her hair was as gray as Mrs. Howard's. He couldn't find any resemblance between both Judiths. Big Judith had the tall, subtle body of a dancer. Frog couldn't have imagined her with a law degree. He wondered how Phipps could have ever thought to tame her. And Holden couldn't help himself. He had the image of Judith Church with her legs around a man. It would have been like making love to a python.

She began the interview, scratching on a sheet of paper with a blond pen. He called himself Micklewhite, which was close enough to Micklejohn, the name his dad had been born with. Sidney Michael David Hartley Micklejohn. But Micklejohn had been a fugitive, and his bosses turned him into Sidney Holden Sr.

"David Hartley Micklewhite," Judith scratched with her pen. "We don't advertise for students. Who told you about the Mimes?"

"Tosh. He's sort of a librarian now, but he studied with you."

"Ah, that Tosh," she said. "And Tosh recommended me."

"He said it was the best training I could ever have."

"But we're Elizabethans, Mr. Micklewhite. We do Shakespeare without words. It doesn't have the slightest practical value. What are your ambitions?"

"I have none, Mrs. Church."

"Then you're a man of independent means."

"Something like that. And I could benefit from the discipline of your troupe."

"And I suppose you'd be willing to make a contribution to the Mimes."

"Of course."

"And what if I said my own fee was five thousand dollars?"

"I'd pay it."

"Then we understand each other, Mr. Micklewhite.

But if you interrupt my classes, I'll have to get rid of you. I won't work with a straggler. You'll have to keep up. . . . Here, you can change in that little closet," she said, handing Holden a body stocking, a battered pair of tennis shoes, and a little cardboard mask.

Holden was bewildered. "I didn't realize we were having a class," he said.

"Why delay?"

He went into the closet, shut the door, undressed, put his clothes on a hanger, and climbed into the body stocking, which stretched around his loins like some extraordinary silken thing. The tennis shoes made a perfect fit. Holden put on the mask, walked out of the closet, and saw his own twins, men and women in dark body stockings and little masks. Judith wore the same party mask with its beaklike bridge. She was taller than Holden, and he could feel her litheness under the silk, like a skeleton with musical bones.

She led the Mimes, and Holden did what he could to follow her moves. Bumping hadn't prepared him for this. He couldn't bend his knees. His body wouldn't glide under the stocking. His chest ached. He was hopeless as a Shakespearian mummer and mime.

He knew *Hamlet* and a little *Macbeth*, but he wasn't sure which country Judith had entered until she slackened a bit and she had all the gloom of Hamlet under her black mask. Holden had come to Elsinore. And now he understood what that farce at the nursing home had been about. The Mimes had staged it for Sidney Holden. He was the audience *and* the big comedian of the show. Dr. Herbert Garden had to be one of the men under the masks. But how had they lured Fay to College Point in Queens?

Holden took off his mask.

"It's been an education, but I have to go."

He dressed in the closet and when he came out, the mummers were gone. Judith stood in her stocking, without the mask.

"We have to settle your account, Mr. Micklewhite."

"You know who I am," Holden said. "I'm not Micklewhite."

"Yes. You're the Frog."

He paid with one of his new checks from Aladdin, signed it "S. Holden, President," and scribbled "personal business" under his signature. He didn't know how liquid the company was, but he refused to worry about Aladdin's cash flow.

"Why did you come to us as a pretender, Mr. Holden? Couldn't you have said you worked for Howard Phipps?"

"You'd never have seen me."

"You're wrong. I've been expecting you. I always like to meet Howard's latest messenger boy."

"I'm not a messenger boy."

"Then what are you, Mr. Holden?"

"It's hard to define. His bodyguard, maybe. And his companion."

"Do you go with him into the toilet when he has to pee?"

"You shouldn't talk about his infirmities like that."

"Why not? He's one of the richest men in America."

"But somebody's been bleeding him. I'd say that

somebody is your daughter . . . with a little help from the Mimes."

"My daughter?"

"Please, Mrs. Church. This isn't Shakespeare. And we're not miming anymore. She calls herself Mrs. Vanderwelle, but her name is Judith Church."

"I'm Judith Church."

"Little Judith then. Are you happy? She likes to play Phippsy's lawyer."

"I don't know Howard's lawyer. What did he say about me?" The bones of her face seemed incredibly fine in the spangled light of the loft. "What did he say?"

"That he loved you. That he was stupidly jealous. That you ran away and got married to a Rochester man. That the man killed himself on account of Phipps . . . and you went into a funny farm."

"Elsinore," she said.

"What?"

"Howard put me in a sanitarium. Elsinore."

"Is it in Queens?"

"No. Vermont. Near Montpelier. It was a deluxe prison camp. A gulag with champagne. Howard visited all the time. I bit him on the mouth. I drew blood. It was like having a year ripped out of my life."

Two Elsinores? One in Queens. One in Vermont.

"Is it still functioning? Elsinore."

"Not unless Howard had other old companions who went berserk. It was much too grand. Every patient with her own butler. Elsinore must be buried under the snow by now. But who told you about this daughter I never had? Not Howard. It must have been your librarian, Tosh."

"Tosh doesn't lie," Holden said.

"Then he lives in too many libraries. . . . Thank you, Mr. Holden, but I have work to do."

"How can I get a ticket to one of your performances?"

"We never perform in public. I'm opposed to audiences who come in off the street. Whatever we do is by invitation only. And I'm afraid you're not right for our guest list. Good-bye, Frog."

"I'm not so fond of good-byes."

"Then I'll have to ask my people to throw you out."

"I still say you have a daughter. No one but little Judith could have told you who I am."

Six or seven mummers appeared from behind a door, like waltzing skeletons. Frog tried to pull at their masks, hoping he'd uncover little Judith or Dr. Herbert Garden. But he still couldn't understand how the Manhattan Mimes had captured Fay and put her in their own Elsinore at College Point. And while he dreamt about that, the mummers seized Holden and tossed him down two flights of stairs. He couldn't even get a single mask in his hands. He arrived on the street with a twisted shoulder. He heard a door click. The mummers had locked him out of their loft.

He went straight to the Phipps Foundation.

Gloria Vanderwelle greeted him outside Phippsy's office. Frog began to doubt himself. He couldn't imagine that girl with the bow in her hair as one of the Mimes. But she had to be Mrs. Church's daughter. Little Judith.

"Mr. Phipps is waiting for you," she said.

"How did he know I was coming?" Frog asked, looking into her eyes.

"He's psychic about his employees."

Holden didn't believe in psychics. Phippsy must have had a secret route to the Manhattan Mimes.

"He's upstairs in the Supper Club," she said. "Having his tea."

Frog rode up to Phipps' crazy Manhattan, that enormous bowl of metal and glass where the conqueror liked to eat by himself. Phipps sat far from the windows, at a modest table for two. He was nibbling on a soda cracker. Frog had to think like a president. The overhead on that cracker must have been half a million.

"Hello, Sid. Should we move to a bigger table?"

"No. This one is fine."

Frog sat down with the old man.

"Would you like a breakfast steak?"

"It's almost dinnertime," Holden said.

"So what? I keep the hours in this establishment. I'm Father Time."

"I'll have a soft-boiled egg, an orange, and a bit of toast."

Holden didn't have to bark his order. The egg appeared with the orange and a piece of rye toast. Five waiters hovered over him, one to open the egg, one to slice the orange, one to bother about salt and pepper, one to supervise the supervisor.

"Damn you," Phipps shouted, "will you let the boy suck his egg in peace?" And the waiters disappeared. Phipps was silent while Holden devoured the egg.

"How's the grub?"

"Good."

"We have to get back on the road. It's Europe this time, Sid."

"More funny paper?"

"Ah, you've been reading my mind."

"But the other swag we collected was good as gold."

"Who told you?"

"I swiped one bill and had it checked."

"So I make you president and you become a bloody thief."

Holden returned the thousand-dollar bill. The old man tore it to bits. "I could give you to Paul Abruzzi. He'd love to get his hands on the boy who romanced his daughter-in-law."

"I'm not a boy," Holden said. "And I didn't romance Fay."

"I could borrow a couple of heavy hitters. You'd never leave this building alive."

"Probably not. But I'll bring you along, Phippsy."

"You wouldn't dare."

"Call your hitters and see what happens."

"I promoted you and you scheme behind my back."

"I used my wits, that's all. And don't talk to me about funny paper and *the life*. You're a billionaire who happens to be cash poor. How come?"

"There's a leakage and I can't find it. So I have to collect what's mine. I'm too old to run around the world alone. And you're the best collector in the business."

"Aladdin didn't have your kind of debts. Phippsy, why don't you concentrate on the leaks. You have lawyers, accountants."

"They're pissing in the dark."

"Then look a little closer to home."

"What do you mean?"

"Like Mrs. Vanderwelle."

The billionaire froze behind his cardigan in that

restaurant that was like a cathedral. Whatever mercy he had for Holden was gone.

"I told you. She's off-limits."

"But she's the key to all your cash problems."

"You're fired," Phipps said.

"Good. I can go back to early retirement."

But when Frog stood up, the old man started to mewl like a little boy. Then he wiped his eyes with his end of the tablecloth. "Sit down, Sid. Please."

"Not if we can't discuss Gloria Vanderwelle."

"She's my daughter. I told you that."

"But her name isn't Gloria. It's Judith. Judith Church."

"You're cracking up, Sid. There's only one Judith in my agenda. And she runs an acting school."

"The Manhattan Mimes. I've been there."

"You visited Judith?"

"Someone has to look out for your interests. Besides, if you lose your empire, I'll lose Aladdin. And I like being president, even if I can't tell where our capital comes from.

"You visited Judith? Without my consent? Not a word of warning. What does she look like?"

"You ought to remember. She was your woman, for God's sake."

"But I haven't seen her in twenty years. She could have developed a tick, or some monstrosity of the face. And I'd be the last to find out."

The old man seemed miserable, and Frog had to reassure him. "She's beautiful, Phippsy. With a gorgeous head of gray hair."

"Go on. What else?"

"She knows I'm working for you."

"That's insignificant," the old man said, growling again.

"Only one person could have told her. Your daughter, Mrs. Vanderwelle."

The old man stared out of those merciless wet eyes. "Sid, do I have to fire you again? Judith, damn you. Did she mention my name?"

"Yes. She calls you Howard."

"Why shouldn't she call me Howard? That's who I am. Ought to be obvious to a child."

"She said you put her in a sanitarium after her husband killed himself. The sanitarium was outside Montpelier. And she bit you on the mouth."

"I still have the scar. Took a couple of operations to heal that wound. But did she talk about this restaurant? She loved sitting here, surrounded by glass. She'd dance from morning to midnight. Had to keep my saxophones on a twenty-four-hour call. People would line up forever, just to watch her dance. Can you imagine? My competitors thought she was a shill. They hired a woman to haunt their own clubs. But it never worked. Judith was the genuine article."

"She didn't say a word about the Supper Club."

"That was to punish me."

"We talked about Elsinore."

"Bloody Elsinore? What's that?"

"The sanitarium where you put her."

"It didn't have a name. That was the whole point of it. The clientele wasn't interested in publicity. It was a house in the woods."

"Well, she called it Elsinore."

"That's not pertinent to this conversation. Judith has

an inventive mind. What else did she say?" Holden was silent. "What else?"

"She asked if I went into the toilet with you every time you had to pee."

Phipps started to laugh. But the sound was very shallow. And Holden was sorry he'd ever talked about toilets. "She was joking, Phippsy."

"Judith doesn't joke. She wanted to eat my heart out. . . . Come on, Sid. We have to go to Spain. I already booked the seats."

"I thought I was fired."

"Can't fire a president, just like that. You have certain privileges."

The old man got up from the table. And that one gesture brought a fury to the restaurant. Waiters ran to him from every side.

"Stop it," Phipps shouted. "I have my man."

And Holden walked him out of the restaurant.

8

Holden loved the airport at Bilbao. He didn't have any
steps to climb. The Aeropuerto de Bilbao was a bright
little box on a simple plain. The hills outside were
summer green, and Holden saw a cemetery surrounded
by poplar trees. The stones in the cemetery looked like
gray teeth. The Guardia Civil didn't bother him. Holden
had never bumped in Bilbao. It was neutral territory.
He'd bumped in Madrid, which had its own street of
furriers, furriers who'd tried to steal patterns from his old
senior partner, Bruno Schatz. Schatz had arranged Hold-
en's calendar of hits. But now Holden was president of
Aladdin, and he didn't have to take calls from Schatz in
the middle of the night. Schatz had married Holden's
bride, Andrushka the twig.

A red Jaguar was waiting for them in front of the
airport. Holden didn't see any driver. "I warned you,
Phippsy. I'm not your chauffeur."

"Will you get in? I can't have a third party involved in
our affairs. One of us has to drive. Me or you."

"But you're making a habit of it."

"Then give me a better solution. Get in."

The keys were in the dash. Holden stared at the silver emblem of a very long cat. He'd never driven a Jaguar before. Phipps spread out his map of the Spanish coast like some commandant. The map had a leather cover and a magnifying glass. Phipps searched the coast with that glass. "This is Basque country," he said. "The Basques would tear our heads off if they could. The Basques hate everybody except the Basques. They're the only people in the world who never wanted to get rich. That makes them honorable."

"And dumb."

"No. Not dumb. There's a difference. The Basques wouldn't have wanted my Supper Club. They're crazy about bingo. They build palaces for their bingo games."

"I thought they despise money," Holden said.

"They do. But they still love to gamble."

"Where did you learn so much about the Basques?"

"I lived near those motherless sons. A long time ago. I bartered with them. The Basques made me rich."

"Where haven't you lived?" Holden asked. "You're like Marco Polo with your maps."

"Just drive the car, Sid. Just drive the car."

They traveled down the coast, passing tiny villages with beauty parlors and cider houses off the highway. There was odd writing engraved on the mountain walls: *HERRIBATASUNA*. Frog had never encountered such a word. "Phippsy, what does it mean?"

"Pay no mind to it. It's Basque."

They passed a beach that looked like Copacabana. And Holden was reminded of Brazil. He'd followed a furrier there, hunted him down in Rio, a rival of the Swisser's who'd stolen designs from Aladdin. Holden had to retrieve the designs and bump the furrier as a lesson to other furriers. But he never got near the beach. It was in and out of Rio. That was the legend of Holden's life.

They drove across another province and entered the mountains of Asturias.

"Anarchist country," Phipps said.

Holden didn't see any anarchists, just a few donkeys crossing the road and the Marlboro Man painted on the side of a bald mountain. They stopped at a town called Pescadores. It had its own port, a church on a hill, Roman ruins, a tobacco factory, a park named after some Asturian queen, a ramblas, gardens, plazas, a beach, but only one hotel, called Carlos Marx, on the Calle Don Quijote. The Carlos Marx advertised itself with three stars, but Holden couldn't find a caballero to park his Jaguar. There was no one behind the desk, not even a grim-eyed man to inspect Holden's passport, or a boy to fetch him some mineral water without gas. Holden had to bring in all the luggage by himself.

"Phippsy, does this hotel ever come alive?"

"It's alive. But it isn't partial to tourists. The town sort of keeps to itself."

"But it has a beach."

"For the locals, Sid."

"Then why are we here?"

"To sit down with the general. He happens to be holding bonds of mine."

"Who's the general?"

"Forgot to tell you, Sid. He's the hero of the whole

province, but he hangs out in Pescadores. You could say he owns the town."

"And this hotel. What's his name?"

"Well, that's disputable. He lost it fifty years ago, in the Spanish civil war. There was a price on his head. He had his own army, and he was younger than Joan of Arc. Sixteen. They called him Bibo. He shot Franco's men to pieces. He held this town, Sid, until the very end."

"And Franco let him live?"

"El Caudillo didn't have much of a choice. The boy was too damn popular. And how would it have looked for Franco's regime to blindfold a boy general and shove him in front of a firing squad? There would have been uprisings every year on the anniversary of his death. El Caudillo exiled him to this town. And the boy has never stepped outside its perimeters, even after El Caudillo died. But they wrote each other letters for years. I think Franco admired him, as one general to another. But I'm not sure."

"And how did you get involved in all this?"

"Well, I sold ball bearings to both sides during the civil war. But I saved my best stuff for the Basques and the boy general. I was awful fond of Bibo. And I had one or two things on him after the fighting stopped."

"You blackmailed him?"

"Sort of. That's why he's been holding my bonds. Bearer bonds. Any imbecile can cash them in."

"Don't you believe in banks, Phippsy?"

"Biggest thieves in the world, bankers are. Pious too. Wouldn't trust my personal fortune with them."

"Now tell me about the boy general's big sin."

"He pussied around with the Germans."

"After 'forty-one? Suppose he was doing Franco a little favor? The boy's war was over, wasn't it? What else was there for an anarchist to do?"

"Ah, but he pussied around earlier than that. During the civil war. In the thick of all that blood. He was a bit of a German spy. Didn't compromise his own troops. But he fed the Nazis information. That much I know. I swiped a few papers from Hitler's secret service. And so Bibo's been sitting on my bonds."

"And you've come to claim them?"

"Exactly."

"In his hotel."

"Why not? Pick any room you like. No one stays here."

Holden carried the baggage up a flight of stairs. He expected dust and cobwebs and little secretive mice at the Hotel Carlos Marx, but he found none. He chose two adjoining rooms for the billionaire and himself. Some invisible maid must have arrived before Holden did. The linen was fresh. The mirrors had been polished. The toilet was impeccable. The entire hotel had been scrubbed down, room after room. And it wouldn't have mattered which door Holden had decided on. The boy general had been waiting for their visit. He was much too neat for an anarchist.

Phippsy took a nap, and Holden went downstairs into Pescadores. He followed the Calle Don Quijote to a little garden near the beach. The garden was filled with old women who looked at Holden as if he were some sea animal. Holden returned to his room.

The billionaire rose at seven, had a bath, drank a Coke from his minibar, put on a linen suit with a sweater underneath to guard him from a chill, and knocked on Holden's door.

"It's time to meet the general. Did you bring a gun?"

"No."

"That's a shame. Because Bibo already has the advantage of his home town."

"Phippsy, how could I have gotten a gun through the goddamn metal detector?"

"I'm not that foolish, Sid. I could have arranged for a pickup in Bilbao."

"We would have had to monkey with the Basques."

"It's better than being empty-handed. Come on."

They went toward the harbor. Holden saw a beggar playing a bagpipe. He saw gypsy children. He saw fishermen standing on the seawall. There was a cow's head in the water. Holden didn't care. The head seemed benign.

They went up an old, winding hill, arrived at streets whose names had been removed from the walls, and Holden realized: This is how the general likes it. He erases all tracks of himself. Has his own enchanted town, where old women gossip near the beach, and men live out their lives inside the dark of a door.

They entered a crumbling palace. Holden heard the whine of motorbikes. Brats of fourteen and fifteen with rifles slung around one shoulder, and wearing brown shirts stolen from the Guardia Civil, were racing across the general's gigantic living room. Their bikes caromed off the general's furniture. And Holden groaned. He'd had to go up against seventy-five-year-old men in Chappaquiddick. Minot and Paul. And now he'd have to face an army of children with carbines and bad teeth.

The general met them in his library. He had a seam
down one side of his face, a long pocket of skin that was
more like an act of nature than the rotten sewing job of
some anarchist surgeon. He still looked like a boy. His
chin line was as firm as Holden's. He smoked cigarettes
with tobacco strong enough to destroy Holden's mouth.
The general didn't seem to mind the roar of bikes around
him.

He'd already signaled to the old man. And Frog
understood right away that Phippsy was closer to the
general than he liked to reveal.

"I'm starving," the general said.

Phippsy grunted at him. "Jesus, it's not even dinnertime. And this is your town."

"I'm always hungry," the general said.

"Bibo, you must have eels up your ass. They're feed-
ing on your blood. You won't find a restaurant open at
this hour. It's not London or New York. It's Pescadores."

"And in Pescadores dinnertime is whenever Bibo
wants to eat."

"But I'll get embarrassed if you start shouting at the
waiters. I won't be able to stand the stress. Have an
aperitif. We'll whistle away a couple of hours."

"Viejo, I want to eat now."

They walked out of the palace, dodging the fourteen-
year-old bikers, who hissed at the general, and Holden
wondered if that was how all anarchists behaved. They
entered a tiny restaurant across from the palace. El
Pescador, with an octopus painted in the window. But no
one stirred for the general. El Pescador was only a
darkened cave. All those years of exile must have hurt
Bibo's grip on this crazy town. He sat in the cave, said

nothing, and slowly men emerged from the blackness.
El Pescador had a barman and a chef. Candles were lit.
And the scar on Bibo's face, that flap of skin, had a kind
of gorgeous color.

"Old man," Bibo said, "what would your bodyguard
like to eat?"

"He's not my bodyguard. He's my companion, Sid
Holden. He's the president of his own company."

"I know who he is," Bibo said. "El Presidente, what
would you like to eat?"

"Paella," Holden said. That's all he ever had in Spain,
no matter what town he was in.

"This is Asturias," the general said. "I would insult the
cook and his brother if I asked him to prepare a dish from
another province. We are soldiers who live near the sea.
Paella doesn't sit well under the heart. I can bring you
some fisherman's stew . . . and red beans."

"Sid asked for paella," the old man said. "I didn't bring
Sid here to disappoint him over a dish."

"I'm starving. Do you know how long we'll have to
wait for his paella?"

"It's your country, Bibo. It's your house. You solve the
problem. We're only guests."

Bibo wailed at the chef in a language that was so
sad, Frog wished he could forget about his passion for
paella. "General, I changed my mind. I'll have the red
beans."

"No," Bibo said. "If we cannot give you the best paella
you have ever had, I will close El Pescador."

The barman arrived with a bottle of cider and three
tall, thick drinking glasses. But Holden wasn't allowed
to pour for himself. The barman held the bottle behind

his shoulder, took Holden's glass, and poured. Half the cider spilled between Holden's legs. The other half splashed against the lip of the tall glass. "Drink," the general ordered. And Holden gulped down all the cider that had gone into his glass. It was sweet as God. His head pulsed with the taste of cider. He couldn't stop watching the barman, who held the bottle behind him like a bullfighter's sword. The barman never broke that horizontal line. The bottle didn't waver once. Holden had six long gulps before the paella arrived in a huge round shallow pot with pieces of cloth stuffed into the handles so the chef wouldn't burn his fingers. "Paella por tres."

"Por todos," the general said. "Honor our table and eat with us."

"Bibo, I cannot sit with strangers."

"But you've met the viejo before. Señor Phipps."

"It's the other one, Bibo."

"Señor," the general said to Holden. "My people are frightened of you. Enjoy the paella. But please don't come here again. You will make ghosts of us all."

"I thought anarchists didn't believe in God or ghosts."

"This is Spain, señor. We haven't come to such perfection. I myself am very superstitious."

Frog dug his nose into the paella pan. The hot perfume of pimentos and yellow rice was driving him insane. He almost didn't want to ruin the mosaic of yellow and green and red. But he was much too hungry. He ate like a horse. The chef appeared with a basket of country bread and bottles of black wine. Holden had never eaten such paella in his life, not in Madrid, or even Valencia where paella was born. There was no glue in the paella pan. Holden could see every kernel of rice. He ate much more than the general. And the billionaire picked at a morsel of yellowed chicken. He was too old to have an appetite, or too depressed, or too worried about the state of his bonds.

Frog didn't leave a kernel of yellow rice in the pan.

He drank three bottles of wine and started to snore at the table. He was still awake, but he couldn't stop snoring. His ears seemed to grow out of his head. He thought of Elsinore and his darling who was lost to him. And then his shoulders dropped and the bumper fell into his own kind of peace, which was like oblivion.

♫

He woke in his room at the Carlos Marx. He was wearing silk pajamas that didn't belong to him. There was a pot of coffee beside his bed. Cookies on a silver tray. A flower from one of the gardens of Pescadores. Holden was beginning to feel like an anarchist. He wouldn't have minded a week in Bibo's town, a rest from Aladdin. And he admired this hotel, with its magic room service. But as he drank his coffee, he could hear someone singing in the courtyard below. He didn't understand a word. But the song was so full of grief, so lamentable, that Holden wanted to hurl himself from the window, give his body to the siren's call. He paddled downstairs in his new silk pajamas, with pesetas in the pants.

The siren was a shivering young man who sat cross-legged in the yard. Something was wrong with his face. His eyes seemed to wander in all directions. He gathered the phlegm in his mouth as he sang. It looked like a ball.

"Please," Holden said. "You can have all my pesetas if you'll stop. I love the song. It's beautiful. But it makes me want to jump out of my skin."

He left his pesetas in the siren's little cup and marched back upstairs to his room. But when he picked up a cookie to put in his mouth, the singing started again. "Damn," Holden said. "You pay and pay and it's never enough."

The singing destroyed whatever chance of breakfast Holden had.

He knocked on the billionaire's door. "Phippsy, it's me. Your servant, Sid." But the billionaire wouldn't answer him. Phippsy didn't like to sleep late. Holden knew that. He walked into the room. Phippsy wasn't there. And he didn't have any coffee beside his bed. Phippsy had never returned from El Pescador.

Frog got into his clothes. He was preoccupied with the missing old man and never even noticed that the singing had stopped. He went down to the Jaguar. The siren was sitting on the hood. He didn't have his beggar's cup. He was wearing a carbine now. He was one of the general's biker boys.

"El Presidente, I have a message from Bibo. He would like it very much if you would leave Pescadores. He has put ten thousand cash dollars in the red car. And he promises to you that no hurt will come to Señor Phipps. He knows you are an assassin, but we can also be assassins, señor."

"Where did you learn your English?"

"Not at school, El Presidente. Bibo is our teacher."

"Then you can tell him that I won't leave without the viejo."

"I am sorry, señor, but I will have to assassin you."

Jesus. He couldn't get Phippsy back without battling an army of children. He blamed himself. No more jobs. He was near enough to throttle the boy's windpipe. But he wouldn't destroy a siren just like that. He pulled on the boy's trousers, grabbed the carbine away, and while the boy rolled in the grass outside the Carlos Marx, Holden played with the Jaguar's gears, shot across the Calle Don Quijote, and drove into the heart of Pescadores.

He could hear the motorbikes converge from different streets. Holden braced the carbine against his window and arrived at Bibo's palace before any of the boys. Bibo stood inside the palace gate. He had a blue bandanna and an ancient army shirt.

"I could have cut your throat last night," the general said. "But I brought you to the Carlos Marx and dressed you in pajamas."

"Why were you so charitable with me?"

"Because I didn't think you were such a fool. The viejo would buy you and sell you if he could. He has no friends. And you are a gunman without a gun."

"But I have this carbine, Bibo."

"A toy," the general said.

The bikers descended upon the palace. The general dismissed them with a growl that started so deep in his throat, half his body seemed to rise up from the gate. And now Holden understood where the siren had learned his songs. Bibo was the best tutor in town.

"Come inside, El Presidente. But without the toy."

Holden left the carbine against the gate and followed Bibo into the palace.

They had their coffee in Bibo's kitchen. They had pale cherries in ice water. They had a thick golden cream.

"She is a beautiful woman, your first wife."

"I was only married once," Holden said. "But who told you about Andrushka?"

"Señor, she was in this house. More than once."

"You met the twig and Bruno Schatz?"

"I've known Bruno since I was a boy."

"General, you were never a boy. But you had German connections. That's what Phippsy said."

"El Presidente, we all worked for Phipps."

"Then why are you keeping him here?"

"Because he wants to rob me of everything I have. And I thought a few hours of solitary confinement might make him more reasonable."

"Is it something to do with bearer bonds?" Holden asked, biting into a pale cherry.

"The bonds are a guarantee for my old age. I have no other guarantees."

"General, you have a whole damned town."

"We have no industries, señor. And the upkeep is tremendous. I have to feed the mayor, his bodyguards, and mine. I have three hundred widows to support, sixteen imbeciles, a horse doctor, two pharmacists, three unmarried sisters, and ten cows. I need the bonds."

"But the old man needs them more. All his assets are leaking. And he has to plug the holes. If he starts to drown, General, Pescadores might fall into the sea."

"Then we are at an impasse."

"I don't think so," Frog said. "General, if you don't

come up with Phippsy and the bonds in five minutes, I will have to pull off the front part of your face."

"I have the army, señor. You don't."

"But your army is blowing wind on a bunch of motorbikes. And my hands are inches from your head."

"You're a hired assassin," the general said. "Do you know how many corpses I've pissed on, bodies I have burnt?"

"It's one-on-one, General. Just you and me."

Bibo looked into Holden's eyes. "All right," he said. "I'll give you the old man."

9

"You're lucky to be alive."

They'd returned to Bilbao, and Holden had gotten the old man on board the plane with his sack of bearer bonds.

"I said you're lucky to be alive."

"And I could strangle you, Phippsy, right in your seat, and cash in those bonds of yours."

The old man contemplated Frog's proposal. It seemed to calm him. "You don't have the nerve. You'd wilt without me. You'd wander inside your head."

"But I wouldn't have to rescue you from some boy general."

"You didn't rescue me. I was having a long talk with Bibo. He was about to cave in."

"Phippsy, he would have stolen your pants."

"Big deal. He let you fall asleep on a shitload of Spanish cider. He drugged you, Sid. And he could have cut your throat."

"Then why didn't he?"

"Bibo's fond of you. You're his baby brother."

"I'm not his brother. I had paella with him once."

"But he sensed that you're an exile, like him."

"He sensed more than that, Phippsy. He knew my whole career. Tell me about your dealings with Bruno Schatz."

"Swiss? I hardly know the man."

"Stop it," Holden said. "You bought Aladdin right out from under him."

"That's his misfortune. He didn't have the hard cash."

"You used him, didn't you? During the war. He traded with the Germans for you. And Bibo ran your errands. You made money off Allied blood. Schatz was your point man with Göring and Goebbels."

"Göring was an addict. And an art collector. I fed him dollars and drugs. We took some of the art."

"My hero," Holden said.

"I promised you Aladdin, and you got it."

"With Göring as my silent partner."

"Göring's dead."

"Well, no more errands. I'm not chasing down bonds or cash for you. You'll have to fix that hole in your pocket."

"After Paris."

"We're not going to Paris," Holden said. Schatz lived there with the twig. Frog married her when she was seventeen, and one more mannequin in the fur market, a skinny girl who'd never gone to high school, who'd cultivated herself in Frog's house and then eloped to Paris with Bruno Schatz before she was twenty.

"You'll have to go there," Phipps growled from his blanket. "You're still my collector."

"Didn't you hear me, Phippsy? No more errands."

"Sooner or later, Sid. You'll have to go," Phippsy said before burying himself under the blanket.

A hot, dry wind rose off the roofs of the fur market. The air turned metallic. Frog sat in his bedroom office at Aladdin. He was with Benjamin Rudin, a wildcat accountant who'd been stripped of all his licenses. Rudin's business doubled while he sat in Attica. He'd attached himself to a family of burglars, and now his fees were astronomical. But he was the one accountant with a "menu" large enough for Holden.

"I want his books, Ben. All of them."

The accountant whistled through his broken teeth. "He could have me killed."

"He'll never know you've been washing around in his waters. I trust you, Ben."

And the bargain was sealed without a "kiss." The accountant was there with Holden, and then he wasn't. He lived like a burglar, moved like a burglar. Holden never left his office. He had sandwiches brought in. He'd stopped visiting the Copenhagen. He paid his monthly charges and never thought about his rooms over Central Park. He was a president without his own proper palace. He still had a closet with cutouts from the Duke of Windsor's clothes. Windsor reminded him of his dad. They'd both been wanderers. They'd both given up the kingdom of their very own names. But Windsor hadn't been a thief.

Benjamin returned in two days. Holden liked that kind of miracle. The accountant had no pencil or pad. He kept an inventory of Phipps' ruin in his head. He could have been humming a musical composition, not the holdings of Howard Phipps.

"Phipps Steel and Tungsten, Phipps Bauxite, Phipps Aromatics . . . he's losing book value in everything he owns."

"Talk my language," Holden said.

The accountant stared at him with all the shrewdness of a man who'd been to Attica. "You're president of Aladdin, aren't you? Then you ought to learn, my friend. . . . Someone close to Phipps is taking from the till."

"Someone like his daughter."

"I never met his daughter. But whatever accountant he has ought to be shot. It's highway robbery, Holden. Nothing short of that. They're moving paper around, and every time the paper moves, the old man drops a million. He's so fucking deep into debt, he has to keep borrowing so he can afford to borrow. I know a lot of billionaires like that. They just keep putting leverage on the banks. But they have armies behind them . . . and I think Phipps' first and last soldier is you."

He was in Paris that night. He'd taken the Concorde because he didn't want to meet Bruno Schatz while he had a woolly head. He got off the plane and took a cab to the piano bar at the Plaza-Athénée. It was close to midnight on the avenue Montaigne, not one of Holden's favorite streets. It was a country of couturiers. The highest-paid mannequins in the world liked to have lunch at the Plaza-Athénée. But the piano bar was dead at midnight. And Schatz, who was near eighty-two, wore a polo shirt and a jacket with exquisite elbow patches.

"Where are all the mannequins?"

"Holden, they never come here at night."

Holden would stop at the Plaza-Athénée whenever he visited Paris with his bride, Andrushka the twig, a mannequin who'd grown buxom in Bruno's arms.

"You're fond of this place, aren't you, Swiss?"

"It's quiet," Bruno said. "And it reminds me of a paquebot."

"Paquebot?"

"Sorry," Bruno said. "An ocean liner."

The furnishings could have come out of some Atlantic liner between the two world wars. Holden imagined Windsor and his wife on a liner like that. A paquebot with a piano bar. But the Swisser wasn't at ease, and he was in his own territory tonight. He ate nothing but half a melon and a few boiled potatoes.

"Did you lose your appetite?"

"Shouldn't toy with me, Holden. Not when you're working for Howard Phipps. Did he arrange this interview?"

"It was my idea. I'm president of Aladdin."

"I didn't have to sell, Holden. Remember that. I gave up the presidency as a favor to Howard."

"You're scared of him, aren't you?"

"Not exactly."

"Why did you visit Bibo in Pescadores?"

"The boy? With his little gang of brats? It was a sentimental journey."

"You're not that sentimental, Swiss."

"But Andrushka loves the Costa Verde. It was a holiday, I swear."

"I know the woman, Swiss. She was my bride, remember? Bibo's town isn't picturesque. And she loves paella, like me."

"Bibo is still a boy."

"And an anarchist general who runs that town like a prince. He has a scar on his face that frightens people. He must have bumped for you, Swiss, long before my dad ever did."

"Go on. He was neutral during the war."

"That would make him a perfect courier. He was your boy in Berlin. . . . Why did you go to Pescadores?"

Bruno Schatz looked up at the maître d' and ordered another dish of potatoes. He winked at the piano player, who smiled at him and returned to Cole Porter.

"I was doing a deal," Bruno said. "Bibo smuggles diamonds for me from time to time."

"But he's retired. He never leaves Pescadores."

"He leaves when he has to. . . . I didn't have a choice. Howard stole you and the company. I was shorthanded."

"I thought you gave him Aladdin. Isn't that what you said?"

"But it wasn't your usual gift. I was Howard's protégé. He discovered me, Holden . . . on a paquebot. I was selling lemonade between Rotterdam and New York, romancing the ladies. Howard backed me in a couple of ventures, and here I am, yours truly, the Swiss. I was born in Aleppo. It was Howard who made me the Swiss. Owe my life to that man."

"Then tell me, what's happening to him?"

"He's going insane. We had a marvelous deal. Aladdin was his conduit."

"Did I bump for him, Swiss, and not for you?"

"No, no, he never needed me for that. Mind, he was aware of your talents. And your dad drove him around once in a while. But then he makes you president and leaves me in the dirt . . . and it's not senility. He's sharp. He always was."

"Then why is his empire falling apart?"

"Because he's a wild man. Something must be biting his ass."

"Mrs. Vanderwelle."

"Ah, the little woman with the bow in her hair. She shields him from the public eye. You can only get to Howard these days through Mrs. Vanderwelle. Isn't she his tart?"

"She's his daughter, Swiss. Did he ever mention Judith Church?"

Bruno crumpled one eye and winked at the piano player again. "Of course I heard of Judith. She's the love of his life."

"Well, Mrs. Vanderwelle is the child they had between them."

"Not a chance, Holden. Howard couldn't have kept a secret like that. A mystery child born out of nowhere. I can't believe it."

"She's been ruining Phipps."

"He could sack her, Holden, daughter or no daughter. The man's not an imbecile."

"He's an imbecile when it comes to little Judith Church . . . that's her real name."

"What can I do about it? You're president of Aladdin

and I have to suck my fingers to stay alive. I mean, you were my ace. I could collect any debt with you in the house. All I had to say was 'Holden.'"

"What's stopping you? You can still mention my name."

"Not when you're president. I'd look foolish."

"Then I'll write you a letter on Aladdin stationery. One sentence. 'Be kind to Bruno.' But I want to know more about Phipps. What kind of man was he when you met him in the middle of the ocean?"

"A born detective. There was a little family of duchesses and dukes on the paquebot. But no one could figure them out. They didn't gamble or flirt. They weren't nosy. They sat at the captain's table. And I swooned, Holden, looking at their medals and the mustaches on the men, with every hair in line. The duchesses didn't talk like ordinary humans. Each little sentence was a song. And while we were all delirious over them, ready to lick their feet, Howard sent a couple of cables. A launch arrived and took the whole bloody nation off the boat. They were pickpockets and jewel thieves, sizing up customers during the voyage. They would have had every nickel on the paquebot before the week was done. That's when I started worshiping Howard, the billionaire with Pinkertons in his blood."

"He was a cantor long before that."

Bruno started to laugh. "Howard singing in a synagogue? It must have been a scam. . . . Holden, I'm tired." He took Frog's hand. "Stay here and listen to George."

George was the piano player, and Holden didn't like that silent buzzing between him and Bruno Schatz.

Bruno trotted out the door. George smirked from his bench near the window and Holden could have tossed him through the glass, but the president of Aladdin couldn't afford a scandal at the Plaza-Athénée. Bruno had told him nothing at all. Holden didn't care how many jewel thieves Phippsy unmasked. A cantor had to be behind that image of the billionaire. A cantor, not a Pinkerton man.

Holden sat and watched the piano player. There was a curious duel between them. Frog was the only customer in the house. The waiters had receded into some dark closet. The barman disappeared. Holden heard the clack of piano keys, the noise of some tune that could have drifted off a paquebot when Bruno Schatz had been a boy. He could feel the blue mark of a skirt from the corner of his eye. Andrushka had arrived from the heart of the hotel. She was like some big ripe cat in a blue skirt, sitting beside him.

"Holden," she said.

His knees didn't quake. He couldn't love that ripe cat.

"Does Swiss still have a suite at the Plaza-Athénée for his best clients?"

"No. He had to give it up."

"But you didn't come in off the street. You used the hotel door."

"That's because I booked a room for tonight."

"I don't get it. I thought Swiss likes to be the last man out of the piano bar."

"He does."

"Then why am I sitting here with you?"

"It's a memento, Holden, a memento of our marriage."

"I see. Then the room is for us."

"The one you always liked."

"With the gold sink?"

"Yes."

"And a silver angel on the armoire?"

"Yes."

"Our old room." He wanted to slap her, but he couldn't. Now he understood the piano player's role in this business. George was Bruno's lookout man. He'd signaled to Bruno when Andrushka had come down from her room and stood near the door, waiting to give herself to the Frog. They were their own Manhattan Mimes, Andrushka, Swiss, and George. "What's Swiss afraid of? I didn't come here to hurt him."

"But you can. You're close to Howard Phipps."

"Tell me, Andrushka, did you ever meet Phipps during the time we were married?"

"I don't remember."

"Did you meet him or not?"

"Once or twice."

"Swiss introduced you?"

"I think so."

"And where was I?"

"God knows, bumping people in Alaska or Maine."

"I was never in Alaska," Holden said.

"Does it really make a difference. You were gone."

"And what did Phipps tell you?"

"That I was wasting myself . . . that I ought to live in Paris."

"With the Swiss?"

"He didn't say that."

"But it comes to the same thing," Holden said. "And now you're scared. Because suddenly I'm the new man in the palace. . . . Andie, get the Plaza-Athénée to give you a refund. And go back to the Swiss."

Holden got up, kissed his lost bride on the mouth, walked to the entrance of the piano bar, looked at George, and went out onto the avenue Montaigne.

10

He spent the night at a small hotel on the Place St.-Sulpice, where no one could track him down. His room didn't have a gold sink or silver angels hovering over a closet. But Frog was as anonymous as any commercial traveler. His phone rang at five A.M. He roused himself from a merciless sleep. He couldn't have a proper dream in Paris, not after that city had swallowed his bride.

"Sid, is that you?"

Frog couldn't escape that old ungodly god of a man. "Phippsy, how'd you find my address?"

"It was in my file."

"I haven't stayed here that often."

"Often enough. You should have warned me you were going to France. That wasn't nice. How's Swiss?"

"Didn't you speak to him?"

"No."

"Then Andrushka told you about my trip."

"Your little bride? Haven't had a word with her, Sid. Gloria caught your name on one of my screens. Can't leave the country without Gloria hearing of it. You're plugged into our network, Sid. Part of our life."

"What else is on that screen? Where Gloria was raised? Who her mother was? All the synagogues her daddy played in?"

"Shut your stinking mouth."

"And Andrushka? Pretty chummy with her when she was in New York, weren't you, old man? Did you take her to restaurants while I was doing piecework for Aladdin? Plant a little kiss in her ear? Tell her about Paris and what she was missing by remaining with me?"

"I don't have that kind of power, Sid."

"I'll bet."

Holden heard a whimper. Then there was silence and the old man said, "I couldn't lie . . . she was better off with the Swiss."

"I would have bumped you if—"

"Careful, Sid. Can't tell who's monitoring us. It's an international call."

"Bruno should have been more ambitious and sent me after you. I still might come out of retirement for a job like that."

The old man hung up and Frog went back to bed.

He was tired of rescuing Phippsy from phantoms he knew little about.

Holden was president of a company that never even marketed the coats it produced. His nailers and cutters bent over their boards with a poisonous energy that felt like the beginning of some plague. He signed the checks for their salaries and each shipment of sables and minks.

Aladdin was one more Howard Phipps enterprise, a company that was losing blood. But none of Holden's checks ever bounced. Every month a gang of truckmen arrived and removed the coats. And that was the last he heard of Aladdin's wares.

Whenever he tried to stop the truckers and question them, they simply walked away from the job. Then other truckers arrived, and they wore Holden down with that same sullen silence. He let them keep the coats. But he knew he'd have to become his own Pinkerton man or remain the shadow president of a shadow firm. He followed the truckmen to a warehouse at College Point, a few miles from Elsinore, that haunted asylum where he'd met Dr. Herbert Garden and his own fiancée. He stalked the truckers, waited until they delivered their goods, and then broke into the warehouse, using a little pocketknife to dig under the windowguard. He climbed into a strange fort that held Aladdin's inventory of the last nine months, buried among an enormous pile of costumes and stage sets. Half the world could have been reproduced in those false rooms, with walls that went nowhere, windows that opened onto nothing but windows, so that Frog felt he was looking into some endless infernal box, where devils might have danced with their own children.

He didn't like that catalogue of Aladdin's coats, but he could have lived in this warehouse, felt comfortable among the costumes and different stages. Then he happened to turn his head. He saw five or six of the truckers with their own arsenal. The guns they were carrying might have been props, because Holden couldn't recognize the make or the caliber of a single piece. But he was all alone. And the truckers were big enough to beat him into the ground.

"I'm president of Aladdin," he said.

"You aren't welcome here. You shouldn't have come."

"Then tell me why you're stockpiling all my coats."

"We have orders to deliver, we deliver," their spokesman said. He had the tinniest gun of them all.

"Those orders didn't come from me."

"We don't work for you, Holden."

"But I'm president of Aladdin," he had to say for the second time.

"Presidents mean nothing to us. Can you imagine how many presidents we meet in an afternoon?"

"Let's kill him, Rob," one of the spokesman's accomplices said, a wiry man with enormous shoulders. "For the pleasure of it. Just for fun."

"You shouldn't have used my name."

"But if we kill him, Rob, it wouldn't matter."

These weren't bumpers. They jabbered too much, like infants out of an acting school. "Yes, Rob," Holden said. "I think you should kill me. Just for fun."

The truckers scattered with their arsenal of guns. And Holden saw Mrs. Vanderwelle in the wake of their shadows on the wall. She had another bow in her hair. And Frog still couldn't understand why he felt so uncertain around little Judith. Did he desire her or not? She had all the aromas of a woman he might have adored.

"They're actors," he said. "Members of the Manhattan Mimes."

"They work on a truck."

"This is God's own warehouse, isn't it? And I'm little

Hamlet inside a cuckoo clock. I want my coats back, Mrs. Vanderwelle."

"And what would you do? Stack them in your office?"

"I have salesmen. I see them around. Why aren't they out selling the coats?"

"It's the slow season," she said.

"You're using Aladdin as a dumping ground. You throw in cash, and nothing comes out."

"You get your salary. Aren't you satisfied?"

"No. I didn't become president of Aladdin to preside over its ruin."

"You can always complain to Howard."

"He won't listen. You have him in a trance. I'm not even allowed to mention your name."

"That doesn't leave you with very much, Mr. Holden."

"Maybe. But I still want my coats."

𝒳

The same truckers returned Holden's inventory. His salesmen resigned within a week. Holden advertised for new ones. But the fur market was closed to him. No one would come to Aladdin. The cutters left. No new skins arrived. The nailers had nothing to nail. Holden sat with his inventory. He wasn't discouraged. He was like some mad emperor of sable and mink.

He sent the nailers home. And then he stalked Mrs. Vanderwelle. But she wouldn't go near the Manhattan Mimes. And Holden felt as if his own life were spinning backward, spiraling in upon itself, so that he was pushing toward his boyhood on the plains of Queens, a boyhood with a dad who was hardly ever there. Mrs. Vanderwelle inhabited some of Holden's empty spaces.

She shopped. She worked. She went to the movies, always alone. She was too pretty not to have a boyfriend. It had to be her own design. She was Howard Phipps' secret daughter. She could have had any banker in the business. But Phipps despised bankers, Holden recalled.

Mrs. Vanderwelle didn't eat at Mansions or Mortimer's. She would sit in some far corner of a Chinese restaurant on Third. Holden would spy on her from the window. And that's when he began to fall in love with little Judith. Her isolation troubled him. He wanted to send her flowers at the restaurant, but it would have broken his cover, and he wasn't ready to come out of the dark.

He continued to stalk. His own life had narrowed down to nothing. He existed on the borders of her own stark agenda. There were no friends around little Judith. Not a single rendezvous. He would haunt the places where she shopped. He would visit *her* movie houses while she was at the office with Howard Phipps. He'd never adored anyone from such a distance. And he was out of practice as a Pinkerton man. He couldn't have told you what all her little pilgrimages were about.

She'd call him at Aladdin. "Howard would like to see you, Mr. Holden."

"I'm too busy counting all my fur coats."

What else could he say? That he was in love with her shadow? She would have laughed at him.

He saw a man enter her building one night. Dr. Herbert Garden of Elsinore. Garden didn't stay very long. Not more than five minutes. But Holden was still jealous. Garden could have kissed her a hundred times in those five minutes, or fooled with the bow in her hair.

Holden grabbed him once Garden got out the door.

"Hello, Doctor. How are you? I've really missed Elsinore. A little country home in College Point. I could use the vacation. It's a pity you're not practicing anymore."

"Wait a minute."

"Herbert, come with me."

Garden accompanied Holden to the fur market. They went upstairs to Aladdin and walked through a line of fur coats. Then Frog locked the two of them inside his office. They had tea together and some digestive biscuits that were shipped to Aladdin from a London grocer.

"What's your real name?"

"Garden . . . I swear."

"You're not a medical man. You're a member of the Mimes."

"That's how I earn my living."

"I thought the Mimes never perform in public. Little séances for select audiences. *Macbeth* without words. Who's your sponsor?"

"Howard Phipps."

"Don't tease me, Dr. Garden. Did Phipps pay you to do your little comedy at College Point?"

"I'm not sure. I get my instructions from Gloria Vanderwelle."

"What else do you get? Lots of kisses?"

"She's not interested in men."

"Then what were you doing in her apartment. I clocked you. You were upstairs for five minutes."

"I was getting instructions for our next installation. That's what we do. Installations."

"Like Elsinore."

"Yes. We stage events. Always built around a particular client."

"Sucker, you mean. You put together a madhouse in Queens and waited for me to open the door. The clock didn't start until I arrived. How did you know about Fay Abruzzi?"

"Gloria told me everything."

"But Fay was there. I talked to her."

"No, that was Judith Church."

"Big Judith? Don't play with me, Herbert. I could crack your bones and who would listen? It's an empty house."

"But it was Judith. That's her particular genius. She can mimic anyone on earth, male or female."

"Not Fay. She couldn't do Fay. I would have sensed the difference."

"I'm sorry, Mr. Holden. You saw what you wanted to see. It wasn't Fay.'"

And Holden seized Dr. Garden by the pockets of his pants. "How does it feel, Herbert, to have all that power? To fool around with someone's grief? Were you happy when I started to cry over Fay?"

"It's my job," Garden croaked. "We're illusionists."

"That's a lovely name. Illusionist. Takes care of everything, doesn't it? But I'm also an illusionist. And I could turn you into an illusion in about half a minute. No one would remember you, Herbert."

Frog let go of Herbert's pants and threw him into a chair. "Now tell me about your next installation."

11

He flew Bronshtein in from Paris. The furrier had been
his enemy while Holden worked for Swiss. But now
there were no more alliances. Bronshtein had spied on
Aladdin because he understood the value of Aladdin's
designer, Nick Tiel. Nick had been the Michelangelo of
the fur market before he went insane. Swiss had his own
dividend of Nick's designs, but he'd lost Aladdin, and a
Nick Tiel coat was nothing without the Aladdin label.
And so Bronshtein had come at Holden's expense to
bargain over merchandise. His mouth was made of gold.
He was the richest furrier alive. He didn't need Holden.
But he couldn't resist the idea of getting some Nick Tiel.
And he adored that Holden had paid for his trip.

He stared at that curious forest of coats in Aladdin's
factory. "Holden, you shouldn't display your merchandise like that. You're doing an injustice to Nick."

"Bronshtein, why should I con you? This is what I
have."

"You can call me Solomon, Solly, or Sol. We'll be

partners in another minute. But I can't put so many Nick Tiels out on the market. We'll kill the demand."

"I don't care how you parcel the coats. But I'm not selling in bunches. You'll have to take the whole lot."

"But if I move this many coats around, word will leak. I can't afford that to happen."

"I'll warehouse the coats for you," Holden said. "Take as many or as little as you like."

"What kind of sum did you have in mind?"

"Two million a month. But it has to be liquid. I won't take checks."

"And no one, absolutely no one, will have access to Aladdin's label?"

"I'm giving you an exclusive. What else do you want?"

"My partner to call me Sol."

"Bronshtein, you would have had me killed if you could."

"You were dangerous, Holden. I was doing my job."

The furrier left without a single coat. No lawyer knocked on Holden's door. Holden had nothing to sign. Six messenger boys arrived that afternoon with six enormous hatboxes. Holden didn't look inside. He marched the messenger boys across town to Phipps' private kingdom, piled the hatboxes on Phipps' desk, and handed each of the boys a hundred-dollar bill.

The old man was gloomy. "What's that?"

"Profits from Aladdin."

"Then it ought to go into Aladdin's till."

"Phippsy, Aladdin has no till. I brought you all the liquid I could lay my hands on."

"This isn't a charity ward."

"Who's talking charity? I danced with Solomon Bronshtein. He's distributing the Aladdin label."

"That crook? He's been trying to steal Aladdin for years. You're naive, Sid. I don't think you have the stuff to be president. It was a mistake. Give Bronshtein back his money."

"Naive, huh? Scratch yourself, old man. I made a deal. You're getting six hatboxes a month, like it or not."

And Holden walked out of the office. That old man knew nothing about the homicidal quicksand of the fur market. Frog had Bronshtein and no one else.

Someone stood in Holden's way. He could sniff perfume. But he had hatboxes in his head. "How are you, Mrs. Vanderwelle?"

"You could have made an appointment instead of barging in like that."

"But I didn't want an appointment. I found a buyer for all the coats."

"Would you like to have dinner, Mr. Holden?"

He couldn't say yes. He couldn't say no. "I'll think about it."

"Say seven o'clock. At my apartment. I believe you know where I live."

He returned to Aladdin. He considered ordering a turkey sandwich. He wasn't going to eat with little Judith. She'd engineered that Elsinore at College Point. She was the queen of installations with her own mama as headmistress. And Frog was their clown. He wasn't going to eat with little Judith.

He arrived with six pink roses and one of his Windsor suits, forged by his very own tailor.

She didn't have her bow tonight. Her hair lay on her

shoulders like magical silk. He wanted to press his teeth against her mouth, give little Judith a love bite. He didn't dare. They had dinner at her apartment. Her kitchen was as tiny as a water closet. Her windows faced a wall. She lived in some kind of cozy dead end.

"Who was Mr. Vanderwelle?" he asked over his spaghetti, from a cushion on the floor. The roses sat in a vase on one of her raw windows. Holden enjoyed the desolation.

"A boy I loved from college."

Her whole history could have been inside the string of that sentence. He was reluctant to ask her anything more.

"His name was Charles."

Holden ate his salad and listened.

"He killed himself."

Little Judith had baked a pear pie. Holden kept worrying about Charles. The pie crumbled in his mouth as little Judith reached across the cushions. Their noses bumped. "I've never been with another man." Holden couldn't tell if it was one more isolated island of words . . . or a declaration of love.

She started to bite his mouth. She undressed Sidney Holden. He was utterly naked without Windsor's wool. He couldn't remember being so passive around a woman. What did it mean? He was like some helpless animal in her touch. Then it was Holden who started to bite.

They woke like a married couple. She'd already squeezed some orange juice. They drank it together in that apartment without a view. Holden didn't mind the brick wall. He had little Judith. She was wearing a flannel robe. He didn't question her about the fall of Phippsy's empire. He wasn't S. Holden, president of Aladdin Furs. He wasn't Phipps' companion. He was the boy who'd traveled out of Queens and landed in the country of Manhattan, with excursions to Paris, Rio, Rome, London, Madrid, and Pescadores. He was comfortable in their morning silence.

He watched her dress, arrange the bow in her hair. She handed him a key. Holden bathed and put on his billionaire's suit. He locked little Judith's apartment with his key. A sadness fell over him. He knew he'd never use that key again.

He took a cab to the Flatiron Building. It looked like a building that belonged in Cairo. Holden had never been to Cairo. The Flatiron Building had Egyptian columns and rippled stone that could have been rubbed by a lion's paw. There were hieroglyphics in the walls, stone faces that must have told a story. But Holden didn't have the right key.

He rode up to the fifth floor and searched for a particular suite: THE JUPITER COMPANY. Holden waited until five after ten. Then he opened Jupiter's door. He passed the receptionist and entered the inner office. He saw Herbert Garden. He saw big Judith, wearing the cape of a corporate queen. He saw half a dozen other Manhattan Mimes, in the costume of young execs. He saw an older man, Herman Branley, the bauxite baron, one of the last allies Howard Phipps had left. Holden recognized him from a portrait in *Manhattan,inc.*

"Mr. Branley, whatever they're peddling, don't believe it. They want you to hate Howard Phipps."

Branley tightened his silver eyebrows. "Do I know you, sir?"

"I'm Sidney Holden, president of Aladdin Furs. We're specialists in sable and mink."

"I have nothing to do with sable," Branley said. But while he moved his lips, the Mimes closed their little shop, stuffing all the contents on their desks into brief-cases, and disappeared.

"I don't understand," Branley muttered. "I don't understand. I thought I was . . ."

The entire suite had been picked clean. Could Frog tell Branley that he'd broken up one of big Judith's installations? That Herbert Garden had become his own little spy? It would have taken a month, and Branley would never believe him.

"Who are these people?"

"Swindlers, Mr. Branley. They're employed by Howard Phipps' competitors."

"And you, sir. You're president of . . ."

"Nothing really. I'm just a Pinkerton man."

"I thought so," Branley said.

The Kronstadt Case

12

He felt orphaned, sitting alone at Aladdin Furs. Then his bumper's intuition came back. Mrs. Vanderwelle had given Holden her key a little too fast. He hadn't met any bauxite barons. "Branley" was one of the Mimes. The installation he'd broken up had been staged for Frog. Another Elsinore. He returned to little Judith's flat, convinced the key he had would no longer fit the lock.

He opened the door. Little Judith was inside.

"What took you so long?" she said. Her mouth was red as midnight. She didn't look like a foundation lawyer. She was some kind of sweetheart. But Holden couldn't tell. He was never wise around women.

"You stuck Herbert Garden in front of my nose, didn't you? He led me to the Flatiron Building like a dog."

"But you wanted to be led. It's part of your nature. How did you ever survive so long?"

"I'm bulletproof. . . . Was it much of a burden, Mrs. Vanderwelle, making love to Phipps' chauffeur?"

"You're not a chauffeur," she said.

"And I suppose you're not little Judith Church."

"Yes, I am Judith."

"Then why do you go around calling yourself Gloria Vanderwelle?"

"That's my privilege, isn't it, Holden? . . . Gloria's my middle name. And it wasn't a burden making love to you. I rather liked it."

"I'm glad," Frog said, growing very bitter. "What was that nonsense at the Flatiron Building all about?"

"We were testing you. My mother said you'd never wake up. But she was wrong."

"And were you testing me when you staged that scene at College Point?"

"No. That was Howard's idea. He likes to manipulate people. My mother works for him. Or haven't you figured that out? It was Howard who financed her acting company. Should I tell you how many people we've ruined for Howard—with Mother's installations?"

"And now you're ruining him."

"Yes."

"I'm speechless," Holden said. "You can't have much respect for me if you don't even deny it."

"We're ruining him, bit by bit."

"But he's your dad."

"Would you like to guess where I was born?"

"What difference would that make?"

"I was born in a madhouse where Howard put my mom."

"Elsinore . . . in Vermont."

"He would visit her regularly once a week and make love to her while she was out of her mind."

"But the doctors wouldn't have allowed it."

"It was his asylum. Howard owned it. He had it built for my mom. A fortress without high walls."

"And you lived there . . . in the woods with big Judith. Until she recovered her senses. Then she became a drama coach. You go to law school. She has the Mimes. Was it Howard's idea to start the installations?"

"It doesn't matter whose idea it was. We needed an instrument. Howard provided the cash. I waited. I studied Howard Phipps. And then I turned the installations against him."

"Just like that. Wait and wait until you could deliver. But you might have miscalculated . . . about me. I'm a loyal son of a bitch. What Phippsy did to your mom was unforgivable. I still wouldn't betray him."

"Not even for what he did to your own father?"

"Change the subject."

"Turned him into a zombie."

"Change the subject, I said. That's between Phipps and me."

"Holden, there's a man I'd like you to meet."

"Who? Another renegade from arts and archives?"

"I don't think Morton Katz ever served in the army. He's president of Hester Street Hungarian."

"Is that a country club?" Holden asked. "Like the one you built at College Point?"

"It's a synagogue that's gone out of business."

And suddenly Holden was caught in little Judith's web. Because there had to be a cantor in this story. And the cantor wasn't little Sid.

It was one more ruin in a street of ruins. There was garbage behind the gates. Hester Street Hungarian had huge red blisters along its walls. The windows had begun to rot.

Holden was suspicious. He wasn't a connoisseur of synagogues, even though the fur market had its own particular shul. But he had to wonder if this bit of Hester Street was only another installation of the Manhattan Mimes. Little Judith's truckers might have put up those rotting windows and walls.

He entered the shul, avoiding huge chips of stained glass that must have fallen from some window near the roof. He followed Judith down a long corridor that had the contours of a cave. And then the cave turned into a tiny office, with a lamp, a desk, and a tiny man. Morton Katz, president of the shul. Holden cursed the place. Katz had a childish beauty, but he couldn't have been much younger than Phipps. And he had an extraordinary tailor, because the one thing Holden knew was the cut of a man's clothes.

"I hear you work for the philanthropist," Katz said.

Frog liked this little man who didn't bother with hellos. The two of them were presidents, after all. And a dead synagogue wasn't so different from a fur shop that had no nailers.

"I'd ask you to sit, but I can't remember where I put my other chair."

Holden looked around. Little Judith was gone. She'd left him alone with Morton Katz.

"I don't get this operation," Holden said. "If the shul is closed, why do you come here?"

"It's a question of real estate. As long as I'm president,

we exist, with or without a congregation . . . otherwise we'd lose our tax advantage. So I come here every day, Mr. Holden, even on the Sabbath, and sit for an hour."

"And the rest of the time?"

"Oh, I'm never bored. I fool around with stocks and bonds. I reminisce."

"About what?"

"The Kronstadt case."

"I don't get it. Was Kronstadt a firebug? Did he torch a couple of shuls?"

"Kronstadt was the daughter of a rich American merchant. Park Avenue people. She was strangled in a cold-water flat, a few blocks from the synagogue. But it was before your time, Mr. Holden. Nineteen twenty-seven."

"Then why does it keep tickling your head?"

"The case was never solved. And think of the commotion. An heiress found dead. Almost on our doorstep. I felt responsible. The whole congregation did."

"But you're not the police."

"Still, we had to do something. We hired a detective. A Pinkerton man."

"Howard Phipps."

"Yes. He was highly recommended. He'd solved a similar case in Seattle. We had him brought in. Our very first interview was in this office. He was standing where you are now. The same spot. But I noticed something. I was dreaming of a man with a beard."

"Morton," Holden said, suddenly familiar with a fellow president. "I don't get your drift."

"Pinkertons didn't wear whiskers in nineteen twenty-seven. But I saw another face. Hirschele, our Hirsch. It was the same man. I knew it in a second . . . after I imagined the beard. I said nothing, of course. I wouldn't accuse a Pinkerton of having once been the great Hirsch. I'd have made a fool of myself, Mr. Holden."

"I'm nobody's 'Mister.' Just Holden. But who was Hirsch?"

"The cantor, Hirschele Feldstein. Our golden boy."

Boy cantors. Boy generals. Frog felt he was being sold a song.

"Holden," Katz said, "he could break your heart with the simplest melody. You couldn't get a seat at the Hungarian when Hirschele was in town. Millionaires knocked on our door. Gentiles, Holden. Not Jews. They were dying to hear Hirschele sing. Hester Street became their opera house . . . and Hirschele had a child's beard. He was maybe fifteen. And already he had managers and booking agents. Every synagogue in America wanted the great Hirsch. And those that couldn't afford him would have killed to have Hirschele for the High Holy Days. Women fainted when he sang the Kol Nidre. We had to mortgage our lives to bring him here. The gentile banks took our blood. But we always got Hirsch. Hirschele was ours. I was a boy when he was a boy. I sang in the choir. He couldn't read music. Hirschele was illiterate. He made up songs in his head. And we followed him as much as we could. We were the children of that child. He made fun of us, mocked our stupidity. But we had Hirsch. And how could I have forgotten his face, with or without a beard? He had a nerve, the Pinkerton. To come here, stand in front of his own choirboy, and pretend he was Howard Phipps."

"What happened to the great Hirsch?"

Morton Katz started to cry. It troubled Frog to see
Katz's shoulders shake. A handkerchief materialized
from beneath the desk. Katz blew his nose. "He became
a pariah. No synagogue would have him."

"Was it women problems?"

"Women chased him. We knew that. You couldn't have
imagined his celebrity. He wouldn't sing on the radio,
like other cantors. If you didn't catch Hirsch in a synagogue, you didn't catch him at all. Oh, the ladies lined
up for him at Grand Central, begging for autographs and
a touch of his sleeve. But Hirsch never sang at any
stations."

"You still haven't told me what happened."

"An heiress jumped out of his window at a Chicago
hotel. A Jewish girl from a good Chicago family. There
was talk that she hadn't jumped . . . that she'd been
pushed. Hirschele was arrested. They had to release
him. There was no evidence. But the Jewish press
hounded the great Hirsch. The satyr of the synagogues,
they called him. The monster with honey in his mouth.
He disappears . . ."

"And shows up at your shul."

"But can you appreciate how daring he was? He must
have known I would recognize him, even without the
whiskers. After all, Holden, he sang here ten, twenty
times. He still had that crazy fever, a cantor's eyes."

"Did Kronstadt also have cantor's eyes? What the hell
was her first name?"

"She didn't have a first name. Or even if she did, we
called her Kronstadt. Because the family was so power-
ful. Her father could have crushed our synagogue."

"How did the cantor react to the case?"

"He was brilliant, Holden. He didn't ask one question. He brought me to dives I would never have known about. We talked to prostitutes, gamblers, pimps. Holden, I'd never heard of a Jewish pimp. That's how insulated we were at the Hungarian. We thought we lived in a world of pious men and women. But our golden boy solved the riddle. Kronstadt had been a prostitute on the Lower East Side. It wasn't money, Holden. The woman was worth a fortune. Call it bitterness, or some dark revenge on the Kronstadt name. She'd been among us six or seven years . . . even before Hirschele fell. And then I understood the itinerary. He was taking me on an autobiographical trip. He was familiar with every prostitute on Hester Street. The great Hirsch must have sang in a whore's tub many times. He must have known Kronstadt herself. Can't you see? Hirschele broke the case."

"I'm a mule," Holden said. "My mind's not as fast as yours."

"He led me to Kronstadt's killer. . . . Holden, it was Hirschele himself."

"You're speculating, Morton. That isn't nice."

"Holden, it's ABC. Hirsch was the delinquent he always was. Taking me step by step into his own black corner, while he laughed in my face. I had no proof. I had nothing. Even if I'd exposed his past, it's not a crime for a cantor to become a Pinkerton. He walked away. And Kronstadt lies in her grave."

"I don't believe any of it," Holden said. "I don't believe in this shul. Phippsy was a cantor, but he never sang on Hester Street. Good-bye."

There was a limo outside Hester Street Hungarian. Holden didn't even have to ask who it was for. He got into the bus. A dark shield of glass separated him from the chauffeur. He was driven uptown to the Manhattan Mimes. He went up the stairs to Judith's loft. They were sitting together, mother and daughter, on two camp chairs, waiting for Sidney Holden. Not even their eyes stirred when he entered the loft, as if he were some petty criminal they had to deal with, one more nuisance in their lives.

"That was a lovely sideshow down on Hester Street. Morton Katz was a little too perfect. The president of a dead shul wearing king's clothes. Talking about Kronstadt, the heiress without a first name. It was cock-and-bull. The murderous cantor . . . I've seen much better scripts."

"It's all true," said little Judith.

"Then I'm the King of Hearts."

"And who are we?" asked big Judith.

"A mother-daughter team. The best in the business."

"That's flattering, Mr. Holden."

"It wasn't meant to be. You lie and lie and lie. The both of you."

"We've had practice," said big Judith. "My daughter's first playmates were mad people. And I was her own mad mom. You ought to have asked why Howard never murdered me . . . he could have, you know."

"You weren't an heiress," Holden said. "And heiresses were his thing. But it's all lies. Howard says he hasn't seen you in twenty years. Yet you're supposed to work for him."

"I do. But that was one of the conditions of my employment. That I wouldn't have to see him. I would build fake little sets. I would train actors. I would invent whatever environment he wanted."

"Like Elsinore at College Point."

"Yes. You wanted your Fay. Howard produced her."

"He didn't produce anything except an acting class. You were mumming Fay. You were wearing some kind of mask. How did you manage to get her voice?"

"It wasn't difficult. Paul Abruzzi brought her to us on several occasions. I studied her. I watched—"

"Paul?" Holden said. "Paul was part of the scheme?"

"We couldn't have accomplished anything without Paul Abruzzi's cooperation."

"You're all a bunch of lovelies, aren't you? The woman's sick, and you had her pose for you like a doll."

"She wasn't insane, Mr. Holden. I promise."

"I'm happy to hear that. You had one Elsinore, so you had to build another . . . at my expense."

"It was Howard's idea."

"But the details were yours. Phippsy doesn't have your genius. He's only a billionaire. Tell me, Mrs. Church, if you haven't seen Howard, who was the delivery boy? Someone had to handle the traffic between you and him. Was it a little angel?"

"No. Sidney Michael David Hartley Micklejohn."

"Say that again, please."

"You understand perfectly, Mr. Holden. It was your father."

Little Judith found a chair for Holden, who had to sit.

There was no satisfaction on her face. She was like a guilty sister. And he almost grabbed for her hand.

"My dad was that close to Howard? He shuttled between the Phipps Foundation and the Mimes. A little servant, just like Sid."

Frog got up from the chair like a giddy ghost. He didn't look at either Judith. He floated out of the loft. Wherever he went, he couldn't escape his dad. Why did he bother to grow up? He could have remained a dwarf in Queens.

13

He whistled his way across town in two cabs. Holden never liked a direct route. It was a habit he'd picked up when he was still bumping people and had other bumpers to consider. He arrived at the Algonquin on foot, having abandoned the second cab at Forty-seventh and Sixth. Paul had his own little Round Table where he presided like a prince in a dark baggy suit. The Queens district attorney preferred the Algonquin to the Criminal Court Building at Kew Gardens.

Holden sat down next to Paul, who was with a pair of Broadway producers.

"Hello, Paul. I have a message from Howard Phipps. He says you're not worth the money he pays you."

Paul smiled at the producers. "See you, Bernie. See you, Al. I have business with this young thug. You remember Sidney Holden. He's the one who cleaned up the bad boys from Miami."

"Of course we remember," Al said. "We love Holden." The producers shook his hand and left the Round Table.

Paul's face swelled into a deep red mask. "Try that trick again, Holden, and I'll have you pulled off the street."

"I don't think so," Frog said. "Uncle Howard wouldn't like that. And as long as we're making threats, listen to me, Paul. If you ever move Fay around and lend her to the Manhattan Mimes, I'll give up my early retirement and blow your fucking brains out in this fucking hotel."

"I'm not one of your cronies, Frog. You can't talk to me like that."

Frog grabbed Paul's necktie and twisted it against his throat. "I'm immortal. I work for the billionaire."

He got up while Paul started to choke.

Frog had to see Fay one more time. He went to Park Avenue. He had no trouble getting upstairs. The doorman announced him. Frog was guilty now because he was half in love with that creature with the bow in her hair. But he still had a fiancée, even if she was locked out of his life. He had to see her one more time.

He knocked. He entered. He saw a ghost.

"Loretta?" he said. "Mrs. H.?"

The ghost smiled at him. She was a tall black beauty with a touch of gray in her hair. Mrs. Howard had come back from the grave a little younger than she'd been when he last saw her alive. It was Holden who'd found her corpse, Holden who'd carried her out to the funeral truck, Holden who'd cried.

"I'm Miranda," the ghost said.

"I'm sorry. I thought . . ."

"You've come to see Mrs. Abruzzi. I'm her nurse. My name is Miranda Roberts. You're Holden, aren't you? You visited once before. But we didn't connect."

He was still shivering, because the nurse had Mrs. Howard's lilt, a delicious singsong that made him want to die.

"Fay," he said. "I'd like to . . ."

"Of course."

It drove him wild to watch her walk. Her loins were Mrs. Howard's. He wasn't even prepared to meet Fay.

She sat in her own room, knitting with two enormous wooden needles. "Hello, Frog," she said, as if he'd just come from around the corner. The needles clacked, then stopped, and Frog was already outside her field of vision. He said good-bye, but Fay never noticed.

He was paler than he'd ever been.

Miranda offered him a cup of coffee.

"You'd better sit."

"No, I'm fine."

He didn't cry in the elevator. He had his work. *Kronstadt.* Frog went to the Copenhagen and visited with Kit Shea. Kit was in his basement retreat, repairing a broom. He had the broom handle in an incredible vise and bound it to some straw with a great big bundle of wire.

"Kitty," Holden said to his former spy. "Does Kronstadt ring a bell? It was before your time. But I figured—"

"Nineteen twenty-seven. The bird was found dead on the Lower East Side. We had cops jumping all over the place."

"But you were a kid. You couldn't have been more than nine or ten."

"That's old enough when you're a Westie. I joined the gang at eight. I had my ears to the ground. I could feel every tremor."

"Kitty, what was her first name?"

"Who?"

"Kronstadt."

"Jesus, I'm not a dictionary. I'm Kit Shea. She was Kronstadt. Her throat was stretched. Her face was kicked in."

"Was there a rabbi connected to the case? . . . A cantor, I mean. Feldstein."

"Never heard of the guy."

"He became a Pinkerton and then a billionaire. Howard Phipps."

"Phippsy? He was one of us for a while. He ran rum with the old Stanley mob. He was the best. He never forgot an old friend. I still get Christmas cards from Phippsy . . . with cash inside."

"Did you ever bump for him?"

"That's indiscreet," Kit said. "You hurt my feelings, Holden. You shouldn't ask questions like that."

"I'm sorry," Holden said. "But did he ever talk about Kronstadt? Could he have murdered the lady?"

"Yes. No. Maybe. What kind of answer can I give?"

"But you were around him. Did he like to beat up women?"

"One more question, Holden, and I'll ask you to talk to my attorney, Saul Nimbus."

"Saul died three years ago. I was at the funeral."

"There are other attorneys. I can pay the bill."

"Kitty, you were my man. Help me, Kit."

"I have my own loyalties. I'm not a rat. I always helped you, Holden, when I could. I'm fond of the old man."

And Frog had to let Kitty go back to his broom.

He could have gone to the billionaire. Frog wasn't ready. Perhaps he didn't want to hear what Phippsy had to say. He dreamt of Kronstadt, recognized her face in the middle of the night. She had blond hair and big brown eyes. She was almost as tall as Judith Church. And she haunted Hester Street Hungarian like some lady cantor, singing sad songs in that tomb of a synagogue. Then all the extravagance fell away. She was one more lonely creature who longed to become invisible on the Lower East Side. It bothered Holden's sleep. The cantor had killed her. The cantor had killed her. But Frog stuck to Morton Katz.

He followed him home from the shul. The little president of Hester Street Hungarian lived at a golden-age club on East Broadway. It was a retirement colony amid all the broken roofs and patches of bald land. The Esterhazy Houses, Hospital, and Club. Holden begged to God it wasn't another of Judith's installations. He had less and less trust in the world after meeting Howard Phipps.

Frog presented a thousand dollars to the front office in the name of Aladdin Furs. And all of Esterhazy was open to him. But Morton Katz had turned silent. He wouldn't talk to Sidney Holden. He wore pajamas at the club, not his king's suit. And Frog had to track him down in the toilet.

"Go away. Please. I've said enough."

"I have to know more about Kronstadt."

"There's nothing to know. She lived. She died."

"And she got a cantor's kiss."

"I fed you a story, Holden. I was paid to embroider the facts. That Pinkerton didn't have to be Hirsch."

"Morton, what are you afraid of?"

"Everything," said the tiny president in his pajamas.

Frog wouldn't persecute the old man. "Are you short of money? I can give you an allowance."

"I'm not a child."

And Holden felt ashamed. He walked out of the Esterhazy Houses. But he couldn't let go of Morton Katz. He would stand a block behind Katz on his excursions to the synagogue. And Frog almost laughed. Because on his second hike he discovered a man who was also following Morton Katz. The man had that incredible hunched looked of violence that was a mark of all the Westies. Kit Shea had come out of his basement retreat with a sawed-off broom handle. Holden stopped him when he got within ten feet of Katz and spun him around. Kit raised the broom handle with a surly growl while Katz entered the synagogue, oblivious of Holden and Kit Shea.

Frog deflected the downward sweep of the broom handle.

"Jesus, I didn't recognize you," Kit said. "You shouldn't sneak up on a man like that."

"And you shouldn't go around trying to knock the president of a synagogue over the head. Who's paying you, Kit?" Holden seized the broom handle. "Tell your master that Morton Katz is one of my untouchables."

"Tell him yourself."

"If you hurt this old man, I'll break every broom in your closet."

"I don't scare, Holden. That's why I'm a Westie."

"But I never heard of a Westie dropping a man who's eighty-five. Morton is a colleague of mine. I'm a member of his congregation."

"Get out of here. You're not even a Yid."

"Every synagogue has to have one non-Jewish member."

"You're his shabbas goy?"

"Sort of," Holden said.

X

He couldn't run from the Kronstadt case. He sat in his office, pondering a woman who'd been dead for over sixty years. Why did she seem so incredibly close? Kronstadt had removed herself from her own history, and Frog was seeking a history he never had. Both of them might have met at some vanishing point where time and space were as liquid as a miser's millions. The Mimes could have manufactured the whole story. Who cared? Kronstadt was in his blood.

He didn't have to follow the billionaire home to his nest. Phippsy had no nest, besides the Supper Club. He lived in a tower apartment at the Phipps Foundation, two rooms that didn't even have a fridge. One phone call got Frog into the apartment. The billionaire was in a scruffy flannel robe that could have come out of a flea market.

"Had twenty rooms on Park Avenue, Sid. I inherited them from the Vanderbilts. With five live-in butlers and maids. I was miserable in their company. I prefer it here."

"What if you get sick?"

The billionaire pointed to a buzzer. "I have doctors on

a twenty-four-hour call. My own private emergency room."

"But you can hardly take off your own pants."

"I manage," Phipps said. "And I can always depend on you."

"Why did you send Kit Shea after President Katz?"

Phipps started his crazy cackling laugh. His body shivered under the robe. "President Katz. That's a good one. He's an antique choirboy."

"Was he in your choir, Phippsy?"

"Never had a choir, Sid."

"And I suppose his shul didn't bring you to Manhattan to find out who killed the heiress?"

"I was a Pinkerton. It's no big secret. Sure, Hester Street hired me. A private detective has his following."

"Like a cantor, huh?"

"Or anybody else."

"You knew Kronstadt, didn't you?"

"Of course. That was the whole point of the investigation."

"Phippsy, what was her first name?"

"Frieda. But she never used it. We called her Kronstadt. Everybody did."

"Was she beautiful?"

"No, no. Not like Judith. But she was attractive enough . . . and warm, Sid. Kronstadt was warm."

"How'd you meet her?"

"At some soiree. She was running around with a couple of Irish hoods. I liked her. We got along. I wasn't a Pinkerton then."

"What were you, Phippsy?"

"A fresh kid."

"You finished her."

The billionaire looked at Holden out of watery blue eyes. "I did not."

"Then why Kit Shea?"

"It's old business. I didn't want the choirboy poking around in my past. I sent Kitty to warn him."

"With a broom handle?"

"I never ask a man about his techniques."

"But it's Mrs. Vanderwelle who introduced me to Morton Katz. Why didn't you punish her?"

"I'd like a snack, Sid. Let's go downstairs to the Club."

And Frog went down with Phippsy to that make-believe Manhattan. A full orchestra was playing. Holden had violins in his soup. "It's like a paquebot in here. We could be drifting on some crazy sea. . . . My father worked for you. He was your man."

"He ran errands for me from time to time."

"He was your man. You sat him down in some deep cover. He played the chauffeur . . . God, I'm so stupid. He bumped for you. That's how I got my reputation. People were frightened of my dad. So I became the second Holden. I was educated in a school I didn't even know about. You've been nursing me all along. For twenty years. I was the fucking ghost of a ghost. Why did you take me out of the nursery all of a sudden? You needed a bumper, didn't you? I fit the bill. I was your customized boy. Who did you want me to hit?"

The billionaire sucked on some jello. And Holden thought of Kronstadt and Paul Abruzzi and Morton Katz and his own dad's elliptical life. He figured it was fair to destroy Phippsy in Phippsy's restaurant. But he'd never bumped out of so much pain. It was worse than a vendetta. Because Phipps was almost like an uncle who'd risen out of the ocean to harrow the Frog. Or a granddad. And then Holden recognized two waiters he'd never seen before in Phippsy's womb of time. Their coats weren't any less splendid than the other waiters'. But they were bringing food that Phipps had never ordered. And Holden freed one leg as the waiters dropped their trays and lunged at Phippsy with a pair of knives. The old man never moved or cried. And for a moment Frog wondered if he was caught in yet another staged event. But he didn't have the luxury to search for some essential grammar. Even if the whole scene had been choreographed, Frog had to act. His heel landed in the first waiter's groin. He'd twisted the second waiter to one side, so that the knife fell into Phippsy's flannel shoulder. The rest of the waiters stood frozen as Frog punched the two men into the polished floor. He could see his own reflection. He looked like some angel of death. He stopped punching. The two men crawled out of the Supper Club. The billionaire sat with a knife in his shoulder. He smiled, said, "I ain't hurt, Sid," and tumbled into Holden's arms.

Frog carried him downstairs to the emergency room.

14

He waited and waited for that second delivery of hatboxes with two million inside. But Bronshtein must have
lost interest in the Aladdin label. The coats were never
collected. They seemed to grow like trees in Aladdin's
factory and showroom. Frog had a fortune of Nick Tiels.
But he couldn't get rid of the coats. The sables and
minks had a poisonous skin. He gave up the illusion of
being an entrepreneur. He was only a president on
paper. Aladdin didn't even have any books. He could
scratch "S. Holden" on a check. The check would clear,
but Frog couldn't define himself against a bank account.
And he couldn't crawl outside of whatever comedy he
was in. He could have closed the shop, resigned, do-
nated the Nick Tiels to his favorite charity, but he didn't
have one. He might as well have lived in Beirut, along
the "green line" that separated the Christians and the
Muslims, and all the other warring broods. Holden's
green line was in his head.

He visited the billionaire in his emergency room, a

luxurious suite twice the size of his tower apartment. It had its own kitchen and bottles of blood. Phipps was lying like a wraith in a little monk's bed. He wore the same flannel robe. His skin was so white that Frog believed he was in the company of a death mask. Then Phipps stirred, and something like a tear arrived on that white skin.

"You fool. I never killed her. She was my woman."

"When?"

"Before you were born, Sid. Before you were born."

And the billionaire started to chant in a language that was desolate and so, so sweet. Frog was much too stunned to cry. "You are the great Hirsch."

"Was, you mean. That's how I met Frieda Kronstadt. It was Prohibition. And I was at a rum party. I was pissing alcohol. A couple of gangsters asked me to sing. I went through the whole liturgy. I made love to Kronstadt behind a sofa. I was sixteen. She was twenty-six or -seven. I earned as much money as Babe Ruth. I had mink collars on all my coats. I was a rotten, stinking snot-nose kid. I ate coal in Milwaukee when I was nine and ten. I starved, Sid. And then this music teacher came along, a fallen rabbi who was fond of little boys. Morris Love. He showed me how to warble, how to play on all the registers I had. He was touching me all the time. He taught me the whole synagogue service. I ditched him when I was twelve. I was the wizard of Milwaukee. Hirschele, the prodigy who'd lived on shoe leather. But there weren't enough synagogues on Wisconsin Avenue to keep me in the style I wanted. I fled the coop. I hired and fired managers. I wanted no more Morris Loves. I sang the whole United States. I bankrupted the chief rabbi of Havana in a poker game. I seduced three of his daughters. I was the little prince of Montreal. I began beating women in a drunken rage. Not Kronstadt. Never. I couldn't keep track of all my bank accounts. Synagogues booked me two years in advance. I demanded a dressing room, like an opera star. I knew every significant whore in every town."

"And heiress," Holden said.

The cantor smiled. "Should I tell you how many mothers proposed their daughters to me, how many fathers let me peek into their treasure chests?"

"What happened in Chicago, Hirsch?"

"That's a buried name, Sid. I'd rather you didn't use it."

"What happened in Chicago?"

"I was drunk. There was one more heiress. We were battling on the windowsills. I don't remember her name. Her father was a milliner, the richest in the world. First I said I'd marry her, then I said I wouldn't. She fell. I pushed her. It amounted to the same thing. I wanted her dead. And maybe I was sick of singing. Holden, I never gave one shit about God, and here I was, the holy man, with a black pompon on a big white hat. I'd sold myself to Morris Love. The great Hirsch's balls had been in Morris' mouth."

"You were just a kid," Holden said.

"I don't need absolution from a bumper like you. Let me finish. I got out of the synagogue racket. There was no room for a tainted cantor, no matter what his voice was like. I lost my bookings. Only one little shul in Guatemala would have me. I punched around, shaved my beard, and joined the Pinkertons. I solved a couple of big cases. But I was always singing to myself, humming my own synagogue service while I was tracking down jewel thieves for some client. And then the officers of Hester Street put in a call for the hot detective. Don't think I didn't laugh. They'd banned me from their shul. I could have a little revenge and solve the Kronstadt case . . . not for them, Sid. Not for them."

"But Morton Katz recognized you right away."

"Only because I wanted him to. Jesus, Sid, I was a Pinkerton. I could have powdered my face. I knew the choirboy would be on the synagogue's reception committee. I let him tag along. We visited whorehouses together. He blushed like a Jesuit, but he was all eyes. I played 'bow and arrow' with him. I was the hunter. He was the imbecile choirboy. Took me a day and a half to discover who had murdered Kronstadt. But I didn't tell Katz. I pretended to continue the search . . . with Morton the detective. He saw the link between Kronstadt and his hero, Hirsch. He got sadder and sadder, thinking I was the maniac of Hester Street."

"Well, who killed the heiress?"

"A pimp. Marcus Reims. He was in love with her. Kronstadt wouldn't have him. She humiliated Marcus at some café. Could have been the Garden Cafeteria. I'm not sure. She slapped his face. Marcus followed her home and ripped her to death. And so I returned the favor, right under Katz's nose. Had a little party with Marcus. Just me and him. I returned to Seattle and resigned from the Pinkertons. Then I got rich."

"And you fell in love with Judith Church."

"I had my Supper Club and Judith. She ran away."

"You destroyed her husband, she got ill, and you put her in Elsinore."

"We were talking about Kronstadt. Judith's not your business."

"You raped her, didn't you, old man? In front of all your big doctors."

"Shut your mouth, Sid."

"You were the billionaire, and she was the mad lady in your private farm. . . . I think you made up this Marcus. That's what I think."

"Just ask any of the Westies about Marcus Reims. I ended his life. That's a fact."

"And Judith gave birth at Elsinore . . . she had a little girl."

"I told you once. Shut your mouth."

"What are you going to do, old man? Hire Kit and his broom handle. He'd never get near me. Judith Church had a daughter in Vermont. She grew up to be Mrs. Vanderwelle. They bleed you, and you let them. Why?"

"It's piss in a bucket. It's hayseeds."

"Your collateral is going down and down because of them. They're robbing you blind."

"It's piss, I said."

"You're hallucinating, old man. Why won't you talk about little Judith?"

"I saw her once," the cantor said, biting his fist. "She was a month old, but she wasn't my baby. Judith was sleeping with every bummer and bulldog at the place. To spite me, Sid. No, I didn't want to look at that child. I fired the whole staff. I brought in new doctors, loyal to me."

"And you never slept with her at Elsinore?"

The cantor rubbed his eyes. "I might have . . . once or twice. I wouldn't rape her, Sid. She was willing, all right."

"She might not have recognized you. You could have been anybody, a doctor, or one of the bulldogs."

"Oh, she recognized me, Sid. She cackled my name, bit me on the mouth. Didn't touch her after that. Months and months went by, and next thing I know she's big around the waist. I didn't want to look at that baby. Oh, I wouldn't abandon the child. I paid for her schooling like a proper dad . . . and then she shows up one bloody afternoon. At the foundation. Calls herself Mrs. Vanderwelle, but I'm no fool. And I had a pain in the heart, just as if she'd been my own lost child. Little Judith, you say. Let her be little Judith. Short in the legs, with a bow in her hair. Didn't have her mother's graces. But I had to keep from blubbering, because she was my girl in a way. I was the fist behind whatever father she had. I loved her, Holden. I never really understood what it meant to be a dad. I was crazed with worry. I thought of that red baby in the woods, a month old. I should have sung her to sleep with a cantor's lullaby. I couldn't. Of course she hates me. And I let her and her mama eat me alive. But that's what my millions are for. My accountants repair the damage. . . . Holden, the leakage is someplace else."

"Like where?"

"Aladdin."

"I don't get it."

"It was a laundering operation, Sid. It always was. Just like most of the portfolios at the foundation. I never made money on Nick Tiel."

"Wait a minute? You were behind the Swisser all these years?"

"I bankrolled Aladdin. It was my baby."

"And Swiss was only the middleman. I had a boss and I never knew about it. I bumped for you, didn't I? You arranged all the hits."

"Not every single one," the cantor said. "Say seventy-five percent."

"That's because you had other bumpers, like my dad."

"I was very selective with Holden Sr. I only used him in a pinch."

"How would you define a pinch, old man?"

"Like right now. Swiss and Bronshtein and Bibo are working together, pulling, pulling from my accounts. That's why I went to Spain. It had nothing to do with bearer bonds. I had to feel Bibo out. He's joined the Swiss all right."

"Then why didn't he kill you . . . and me?"

"He's the king of Pescadores. And a king could be a little generous. But he's wrong. I've been shutting down his territories ever since we got back."

"And what about the trip to Chappy?"

"I had to see if the Cardinales were involved with Swiss. But Ethan is senile. And so are his sons. I was never interested in their money."

"Then all that talk about funny paper was a big joke. I was your stupid cavalier."

"No, Sid. My insurance policy. I couldn't come with an army. It would have given my hand away. I had you."

"Had me, huh? You gutted my dad, you took my wife from me, gave her to the Swiss, and encouraged Paul Abruzzi to lend my sweetheart to Judith Church."

"I had to get her out of your system. She was always having breakdowns, Sid."

"That's a lot of crap. You figured I'd never go on the road with you if Fay was around. So you had Paul grab her from me. It was your idea."

Holden had to keep himself from smashing the cantor in his monk's bed. His mouth started to twitch.

"Go on," the cantor said. "Do it. I'd rather be bumped by a real bumper than Bibo's little shits. They'd botch the job. And I'd be an invalid for the rest of my life."

"What the hell did you want with me, old man? Why did you bring me out of retirement?"

"Ain't it obvious, Sid. Bronshtein, Bibo, and the Swiss need handling, Holden style. I'd include Swiss' bride in the package, but I know you're sentimental about the twig. I am too."

"She's not his bride," Holden said. "She's a bigamist."

"No disparagement intended. None at all. She's been meddling, but I'll forgive her. Holden, it's Bibo or me."

"Afraid of the boy general?"

"I'm talking business, not the shakes."

"Well, I'm not buying your little package. You can dance with Bibo all by yourself."

"Then kill me, Holden. End it here. I'm your employer. I'd like the job done."

"I couldn't bump a cantor," Holden said. And he left the emergency room. But there were funny people outside, men in surgical masks and hospital gowns. And Holden wasn't crazy about their eyes. They must have been MDs from some forbidden synagogue or school where healing wasn't much of an art. He could imagine the kind of hardware they had under their gowns. He wasn't going to leave the cantor to them. Phippsy wouldn't survive the night.

He found an office with a phone, two floors above the foundation. He got little Judith on the line. "I want to hire you and your mama. I need an installation."

"You can't afford us, Holden."

And he had to whisper around all the masks who paraded in front of the door, winking at Holden, because they had all the time in the world. Holden returned to the emergency room.

"Changed your mind, Sid?"

"Quiet." The monk's bed had no wheels, and Holden couldn't trundle the cantor around, use the bed as a battering ram. The masked men serenaded Holden from the other side of the door. But they couldn't warble like a cantor. There was too much bile.

"El Presidente, we're waiting for you. Bibo sends his love."

All right, Holden thought, there were worse ways to die than in the company of a cantor.

"Phippsy, sing for me."

"I can't. My voice is gone."

"I never admired your millións. Or the Supper Club. . . . Morton Katz is a lucky devil. He sang in your choir."

"Singing won't get us out of here, Sid."

"It's hopeless. I can't carry you on my back. And Bibo has a dozen men in masks. With automatics under their gowns. I might sock a couple. I might squeeze their necks. But I couldn't bring you out alive."

The door opened and Holden saw a little circus of policewomen. The Manhattan Mimes. With pistols and badges and hair in ponytails under their hats. Holden could swear a few of the women were men. That was Judith's genius. To scare these phony doctors with lady cops. They were all roly-poly in their big black shoes. Judith had given them that perfect pitch of menacing clowns. Even Holden was worried, and he understood who they were.

The tallest clown must have been Judith. How much could he tell from her taut, rubberized face? Was she staring at the cantor? Holden wasn't sure. The cantor couldn't have known what these crazy policewomen were about. And then Frog did catch Judith's eyes. She was looking at the great Hirsch as if he were some kind of pet snake. Love, Holden thought. Love itself was a snake. A little garter snake that could bite like the Devil.

The masked doctors were gone. The presence of so many Mimes in police uniforms had driven them out of the building. Frog dressed the cantor.

"Where are we going, Sid?"

"Where it's safe."

"But this is all mine. I'm the king here."

"That's the problem. You're an easy target. Too many people know about you."

The policewomen accompanied them to the elevator, handcuffs dangling from their trousers like obscene toys. Little Judith was in the lobby. Frog had to laugh. His phone call hadn't brought the Mimes. Little Judith must have prepared this installation long before Holden got on the line.

He stepped around the cantor for a moment to whisper in little Judith's ear. "It's complicated, isn't it? Your affairs with Phippsy. You ruin him and you save his life."

"I work for Howard Phipps."

"Yeah, his lawyer lady. You want him hurt but not dead. I'm in the middle of some weird romance. And Mrs. Vanderwelle, I don't like it."

Then he took Hirschele away from the Mimes. "Thank you, but Mr. Phipps is my responsibility now."

He shoved the cantor into a taxicab. They drove north, then Frog switched cabs and shuttled downtown. The journey was like a row of jagged teeth. They arrived at the Esterhazy Houses in their sixth cab.

Frog created a furor at the front desk. The nurses wouldn't admit a new patient off the street. Frog scratched a check for three hundred thousand dollars. He knew now that he could never bankrupt Aladdin. Aladdin was one more of the cantor's money drops. Dollars flowed in and out, in and out, and Frog's checkbook was irrelevant to the whole machine.

The head administrator of the golden-age club pondered with the check in his hand. "But he has no references."

"I'm telling you, this is Hirschele Feldstein, the foremost cantor of his era."

"Holden," the cantor muttered. "Shut your mouth. You're giving my secrets away."

"I do recollect a cantor named Hirsch," the administrator said. "But he can't bully his way in here . . . even with your donation. I need a reference."

"Then call Morton Katz, for Christ's sake."

Morton appeared in his pajamas.

The administrator appealed to him. "Is this the cantor Hirsch?"

"No," Katz said.

The administrator returned the check, his face a shallow color.

"Morton," Holden said, "look again."

"This isn't Hirsch," Katz said.

The cantor smiled, cleared his throat, and started to sing some aria out of the synagogue service. Or at least Holden thought it was an aria. The melody froze him to the floor. Morton fainted. The nurses blew air into his mouth.

The administrator seized the check.

"Hirschele," Katz said, terrible tears in his eyes.

The cantor stopped singing. "Choirboy," he said. "You could never follow a tune."

And Holden slipped out of the Esterhazy Houses.

15

Frog went back home to his office. He had a rage, but against whom? The cantor? The Mimes? Little Judith? It was twilight hour at the fur market. There wasn't a soul out on the streets. He entered Aladdin with his own key. Frog's fur coats were missing. The forest had been picked clean. He knew it was no ordinary burglar. And Frog was without a .22 long to pop whoever had to be popped.

"Bronshtein," he said, "come on out."

The furrier emerged from Holden's office with half a dozen jackals. Frog could read their eyes. They were the same phony doctors without masks.

"Bronshtein, where's my two million for this month?"

"Holden, your accounting is rotten. You ought to think of your own life."

"I'll think about it later. Where's my money, please?"

"I'm surprised you didn't catch on to my hatbox trick. Did Howard accept the hatboxes?"

"No."

"Because he knew they were filled with funny paper."

"I'm speechless," Holden said. "Everywhere I go I walk into a swindle."

"Holden, you swindled yourself the day you started working for Howard Phipps."

"Don't preach. Just tell me how you got into my office."

"Money," Bronshtein said. "It works miracles. Everybody is bribable. Except maybe you and your dad."

"Leave my dad out of this."

"Holden, Holden, he was a very great artist, your dad. I shivered while he was alive. I offered him millions and a Swiss chalet. But he died a chauffeur."

"Bronshtein, I'm sick of talking. Tell your jackals to shoot."

"We're not assassins. Bibo thinks the world of you."

"I'd be happier if he liked me less. And why does he send such animals to attack Phipps in his own building?"

"Howard didn't leave us much of a choice. All our pacts mean nothing to him. We sweat and he sits in his Supper Club. He ought to retire. We can't be his boys for the rest of our lives."

"He's not even ninety," Holden said. "And you shouldn't have made a move on him."

"Holden, he's the one who made the move. He bought Aladdin out from under Swiss. He comes to Pescadores with his new canceler, asking for bonds. He withdraws cash from all our French accounts. I've had to shut two of my fur shops."

"Don't cry. You have another fifty. And all of Aladdin's

coats. . . . Bronshtein, if you wanted to chat, why didn't you come alone?"

"In the middle of a war? I couldn't take the chance. Have I threatened you, Holden? Have I hurt you? I had to join up with the Swiss. Howard's been brutal. Holden, you can reason with him. He can't walk through us like a hurricane and expect us not to fight back. Howard has a daughter, I hear. A certain Mrs. Vanderwelle. Illegitimate, but a daughter nonetheless. We'll be obliged to—"

Frog slapped Bronshtein on the mouth. The jackals drew their guns and grinned. "Good-bye, El Presidente, good-bye, good-bye."

"No," the furrier said with a handkerchief over his mouth. "No violence. Not today."

"Bronshtein, maybe you hooked yourself to the wrong star. Bibo got ambitious. And you figured to stuff the old man, give him heartburn for his ninetieth birthday. He was having some money problems, so you got together with the Swiss and decided to pounce. And you were my favorite furrier. . . . Get the hell out of Aladdin. And take your dogs."

The furrier left, and Holden's teeth started to chatter. He wasn't frightened of Bibo. Whatever revelations Frog had about his dad were like a lousy dream. He couldn't have had a career without Holden Sr. His dad was the prince of bumpers, a man who never circulated much. And Frog had his picture in *Vanity Fair*.

He went uptown to little Judith. She wasn't home. Frog visited her Chinese restaurant on Third, figuring he'd grab a midnight meal. But he didn't have to eat alone. Little Judith sat at her window seat, looking forlorn. She didn't seem like some architect or general who could hurt or help the cantor according to her own calendar. She had Frog's whole history in her computers at the foundation. She could summon up the cantor's enemies, friends, associates, and silent partners. Frog wondered what the printout would be on his dad.

He joined Judith at her table. She was having lobster Cantonese. "The kitchen just closed," she said. "But I'm a regular. I can ask them to prepare something for you."

"Not hungry," Frog said. "Do you always eat alone, Mrs. Vanderwelle?"

"You know my habits. You've been following me around long enough. Besides, I have a beau."

"Who's that?"

"Sidney Holden."

Frog touched his lip. He wasn't clever enough to contain little Judith. "We spent one night together."

"You're still my beau. That's the way I'm built. When I like a man, I can't let go."

"I thought you haven't been with anyone but your husband."

"Not until I met you."

"Can we stop this?" Holden said. "There's a furrier out on the street who's very interested in you. He has six jackals behind him. His name is Bronshtein."

She started to laugh. "Bronshtein of the hatboxes. He's harmless."

"Mrs. Vanderwelle, I know my business. It isn't smart to have a window seat. Suppose I was one of the jackals and I snuck up on you like this."

"Holden, you wouldn't have a chance." She pulled a .22 long out from her lap, with a silvered grip, the kind of gun Frog might have used.

"I've dealt with Bronshtein," he said. "The man can be dangerous. How did Bronshtein meet your father?"

"No one knows who my real father is, not even my mom."

"I wasn't trying to be technical. I need a fix on Bronshtein. Did he meet Howard on some paquebot?"

"You're confusing him with the Swiss. He was a petty criminal in Alsace until Howard picked him up and turned him into a furrier with a Parisian address."

"Another one of Phippsy's protégés."

"He betrayed Howard several times."

"And you? What the hell is your relationship with Howard Phipps?"

"I keep him alive . . . and wound him as often as I can."

"Maybe you like him more than you think."

"No. It isn't much fun wounding a dead man."

"And what happens after you leak all the liquid out of him? Will you defend him in bankruptcy court like a good little girl?"

"I might," she said, "if he can still pay my salary."

"I'd pay it with an Aladdin check," Holden said, reaching across the table to grab her hands. "He didn't kill Kronstadt. He told me. It was some pimp named Marcus Reims."

"You poor Frog," she said. "Marcus Reims is one of the aliases he used. Kronstadt worked with him. Hirschele Feldstein was a cantor and a thief."

"Jekyll and Hyde," Holden said. "I don't believe it."

"It was very pragmatic," Judith said. "He'd come to a town with his beard, play the pious man, sing until all the widows wept, and run from the synagogue to the local whorehouse . . . that's where his passion was. He'd drink, gamble, talk to safecrackers."

"I don't believe it. With a voice like that he didn't have to steal."

"You have it ass backwards. Singing was his cover. He was a thief when he was nine or ten."

"And Kronstadt died because of that?"

"Holden, I can't bring back nineteen twenty-seven."

Frog lost his grip. Little Judith was the one who had him by the hands. She pulled him out of his chair. Her mouth was next to his. Jesus Christ, they were in front of the window. An amateur could have shot out his lights. Frog had never kissed in the Chinks'. The bow fell out of her hair. Love's a garter snake.

He wasn't going to spend another night with little Judith, not until he settled things with Bibo. If the cantor was Marcus Reims, Frog would deal with that too. But Bibo came first.

"Come home with me," Judith said.

"I can't."

Her lips were inside his ear, and when she spoke, his head felt like a horn.

He wasn't sure if the Carlos Marx had a fax machine. And so he sent a cable to Bibo, in care of the Calle Don Quijote.

GENERAL, WE HAVE TO MEET.

Frog didn't have to wait very long. A note arrived under Aladdin's door.

You can find Bibo at the Carlton in Bilbao. Monday next.

He booked a ticket one way. He wasn't trying to conserve Aladdin's money. Frog had no sense where he'd be next.

A Cantor's
Lullaby

16

He woke like a dead man in a dormitory of dead men.
Good, he thought. I've crossed the goddamn river and I
still have all my bones. He didn't have to fear dying
anymore. He didn't have to wake at three in the morning
and start to shiver, thinking what his death rattle would
be like, and worse than that: the irrevocable nothingness
beyond the rattle. If he could *feel* his own death, then
death didn't matter. He could go on planning whatever
mischief he had in mind. He was the same Hirschele
Feldstein Phipps. He wondered if he would have to
seek nourishment as a corpse. Could he suck the salt on
his fingers and call it a meal?

Then he saw the choirboy's face near his bed and he
groaned, realizing now that he hadn't crossed any rivers.
It was the stupidest speculation. He would have to fear
dying all over again. Sid Holden had brought him to the
Esterhazy Houses. With all his millions he was a com-
mon boarder at a golden-age club.

"Choirboy, what the hell do you want?"

"You are the great Hirsch. I didn't see a ghost."

"Would it make any difference?"

"I can't sleep," said Morton Katz. "Kronstadt has been speaking to me for sixty years."

"You never even met the lady."

"But I can't help it if I hear her. She has a voice."

"Shut up about Kronstadt. I have memories."

"I know," Katz said. "You killed her."

"Are you sure you want to say that out loud, choirboy? I have friends in high places . . . and I could hire a couple of lowlifes to kick your teeth in."

"Granted, but how would it change things?"

"Go on. Tell me you haven't been able to sleep for sixty years. I love that, choirboy. Because if I made you miserable, it means a lot."

"You were my idol."

"But the Hester Street Hungarian still wouldn't let me sing in their precious shul."

"We couldn't," Katz said. "On account of the scandal."

"A woman falls out the window, and I don't exist as a cantor? Is that justice, choirboy?"

"No, but it's the conservative nature of synagogues."

"Ah, I'm better off with my millions. People tire of cantors. My voice could have cracked, and I would have had to make my living in the minor leagues. I might still be singing in Des Moines. Or the game room at Esterhazy Houses. Choirboy, get me out of this dump."

"I can't. Mr. Holden signed you in."

"He doesn't have my power of attorney. He's a hireling, a pencil I shove from place to place."

"But he must have had a reason to bring you here. He's a sensible man."

"Choirboy, you talk like the president of a shul."

"I am the president," Katz said.

"That figures. Now go to bed. You're blocking my view of all these fine old men."

"But we have to talk about—"

"Go."

Morton Katz shuffled to his own station. The cantor started to cry. He was forever crying these days. He'd plotted his entire life just so he wouldn't have to end up at an old-age home, and here he was, thanks to Sid Holden. Hiding out at Esterhazy, among the feeble and the lame. If he stayed here long enough, they'd lose his ticket, and not all his millions could buy him out of this place.

There wasn't much of a line to Hirschele's existence. No matter what he accumulated, he felt poor. He'd never left that coal bin in Milwaukee. His Supper Club was only an extension of the cellar, thirty floors above the ground. This cavern had a little sunlight, but he'd rather suck on coal.

✵

He had a phone installed near his bed. Workmen suddenly appeared, with wires, jacks, and cables. They smiled at all the old men. They handed Hirsch small bundles of cash. Pocket money for the cantor. They began to do repairs in the dormitory. They built Morton Katz a cupboard over his bed.

"Who are you?" Morton asked. "Devils?"

"We're from a religious order, sir."

"What's it called?"

"The Phipps Foundation."

And the workmen left.

The dormitory was flooded with traffic, day and night. The cantor didn't stop talking on the telephone. Then he decided to take all the old men on an outing. Morton Katz refused to go.

"Choirboy," Hirsch said. "You can't break ranks. It's not democratic. You'll spoil our fun."

Katz got on the bus that was waiting outside Esterhazy. The bus drove to Little Bangladesh on East Sixth. And that party of pensioners walked into a restaurant called the Bengal Lance. The maître d' was holding a shotgun.

Hirsch accompanied him into the cloakroom. "Herman, you're embarrassing the hell out of me."

"Sorry, boss, but we have to be careful. Bibo's lads have been cruising again."

"Where's your chef?"

"We ran out of food a couple of days ago. I sent him home."

"Then order out," Hirsch said.

"We weren't expecting a picnic, boss."

"Well, I couldn't bring my friends to the Supper Club. I had to close it, Herman. I mean, if Bibo could infiltrate my staff and send two knifers down on my neck . . . I'd have been a dead man without Sid Holden."

Food arrived from next door, and the old men ate downstairs in the Bengal Lance's lower dining room. Hirsch was more comfortable in this cavern. It reminded him of Milwaukee.

The Lance was a laundering operation, like Aladdin. It functioned as a restaurant from time to time. But it stopped pretending while Bibo's men were in town.

Hirsch didn't care about his other "launderies." His own reputation was on the line. He'd promised the old men a decent meal, with tandoori bread and chicken. Not their usual string beans and strawberry jam.

The cantor returned with the old men to their dorm. He liked having them around, even that mournful choir-boy.

The Phipps Foundation was wherever Hirsch happened to be. He didn't need a building or his Supper Club. He was Howard Phipps. It excited him to think of the armada he was sending to Pescadores. He would shut Bibo's town, put the boy general out of business. He hummed to himself. Then a shadow landed on his bed. And all his joy was gone.

"How'd you find me?"

"You've been making too many phone calls, Howard."

The old men had never seen such a tall beauty. They liked the power she seemed to have over Hirsch.

"Sit down," he said, but she wouldn't sit. She'd never come to him before. He'd financed her troupe, but she wouldn't visit him at the foundation. He had to chew a knuckle to keep from crying. He hadn't suffered while he couldn't see her face. He'd lived without the expectation of Judith. But now the pain of his long bachelor-hood returned. He barked in front of Judith like a baby.

"We should have got married the minute we met."

"Oh, yes. You would have cut the ears off every man who looked at me."

"I would have learned to behave."

"Where, Howard? When?"

"I'm not a delinquent," he said, ashamed to have the

old men witness him like that. "Judith, couldn't we go into a quiet little corner?"

"There are no quiet corners," she said. "And you can't lock me in another Elsinore. I'd scratch your eyes out."

"Who's the violent one?" he asked. "Me or you?"

"I had the best teacher. A murderer and a madman."

"Shhh," he said. "You'll give my mates a bad idea of their dormitory captain. I'm responsible for their well-being."

"Always the leader, aren't you, Howard?"

"It's better than sitting in a coffin and waiting to die." He couldn't control his sobs. "Judith, I'm sorry for what I did. Can't you stay with me? I'm not so jealous now."

"But I'd give you a reason to be jealous . . . every night."

"Good. But stay with me."

"Should I climb into your bed, Howard?"

"Here? We'd have to get a curtain."

"I don't want a curtain."

"You never loved me," he said.

"I was your prisoner, Howard, your faithful prisoner . . . for a while."

"But you encouraged our daughter to work for me."

"Our daughter? She has none of your blood. None."

"She's still our daughter."

"Then stop this stupid war with the general. She'll get caught in the middle, Howard. She'll get hurt."

"Bibo wouldn't dare. . . . Why'd you come, Judith? To lecture me after all this time? I pay you a salary, remember? I support the Mimes. I tolerate your little attacks. I let you nibble off a finger here and there. But

I've survived your amputations. And if Bibo threatens all I have, then it's his hard luck."

"I saw you a week ago in your bed. And I was naive enough to think that there was something more than murder in your eyes."

"You were one of those sweethearts, the lady cops? I was groggy, dear, or I would have recognized you. I'll write you a check. You deserve a bonus."

"Howard, go to hell."

And Judith swung outside the perimeters of Hirsch's office-bed.

"Wait," he told her. "Wait."

But she was already beyond the cantor's reach. And no amount of barking and bawling could bring her back. The old men gaped at him. Morton Katz was glad. Because the cantor's crying seemed connected to the Kronstadt case. Katz slept much better with Hirsch in the dorm.

But Hirsch wasn't dreaming of Kronstadt. His chamberlains arrived one after the other. Lawyers, thugs, munitions dealers, and Paul Abruzzi, the Queens D.A.

"You don't have to be polite, Paul. You can ask me how come I'm crying."

"I'm sorry. I didn't—"

"Judith left me again . . . she does it every twenty years."

"I didn't know you'd gotten back together with her."

"She was here, at Esterhazy. You missed her by half an hour. She wanted to climb into my bed. But I had to be a little modest around all these old men. They could eat their hearts out, watching me and Judith. It wasn't fair. How are things in your arena, Paul?"

"I have three of my squads searching around the clock. We'll find those rat bastards."

"I don't like promises. Either deliver or shut up."

"Howard, I'm doing the best I can."

"I paid for your ticket, Paul. I got you elected to the district attorney's table. I opened doors. So don't give me this half-assed shit. Bibo's on the rampage. I want his men dropped. Where's my Sid?"

"Sidney Holden?"

"What other Sid is there?"

"He's not out on the street? I have my sources. They would have seen Holden."

"I'm not interested in your sources. Don't return without Sid . . . and Paul, shake hands with some of my mates. It comforts them to know that a district attorney is in the building."

Paul Abruzzi traveled from bed to bed. He was the cantor's chamberlain, and he smiled, shook hands, made promises he didn't intend to keep.

"Paul," the cantor screamed. "You disgust me, Paul. Get out of here."

And the cantor took to crying again. Where's my Sid? That's what Hirsch wanted to know.

17

Frog needed a package man. He couldn't stroll into Bilbao without a bumper's special. He had to pay a king's ransom for some reliable gun. The beauty was packed in silver foil and was waiting for Holden at the Aeropuerto de Bilbao, under a broken chair in the businessmen's lounge.

He didn't unwrap the silver foil on the cab ride into Bilbao. The town sat in its own cradle of hills. He kept passing little factories. Frog wasn't an innocent anymore. His whole involvement with the cantor had led him to this: a bang-bang with Bibo in the anarchist capital of the world.

The Hotel Carlton was on the south side of the Plaza Federico Moyúa, the central crossroad of Bilbao. Holden understood why Bibo had picked the Carlton for their rendezvous. It must have been the grandest hotel in all of Basque country at the time of the civil war, when Bilbao itself had been the capital of the Basque's own autonomous state. The hotel's burnt-red face had fallen slightly into ruin, as if the Carlton had never really recovered from the Basques' loss of independence. It was a sad hotel. And Frog grew to love it the moment he stepped inside with his silver foil and his travel bag. The lobby was like a great open court where merchants and railroad men and dueñas must have sat, drinking coffee thick as blood.

Frog's room overlooked the plaza, with its green and red circular gardens. The room had crazy little closets, a king-sized mirror, and a safe . . . to protect people's treasure from all the anarchists. Holden unwrapped the silver foil. His bumper's special was a .22 long, like little Judith had carried. It was the same kind of gun he'd used to kill the Pinzolo brothers, Eddie, Rat, and Red Mike.

Frog took a bath in the Carlton's enormous tub . . . without the .22. He wouldn't baby-sit with his own shooter. He didn't think the boy general would try to bump him off in his room at the Carlton. But you could never tell.

He put on a simple gray suit and went downstairs with the gun. There were no messages in his mailbox. And Frog wasn't going to play cat and mouse. Fuck Bibo. He'd find the best paella in town. Even anarchists had to eat yellow rice.

Then he noticed a tourist guide in the lobby. It didn't seem right for Bilbao. The Basques weren't that fond of tourists. They wouldn't have bothered to advertise themselves. The guide wore a very old shirt. His cuffs were frayed. His parrot-green jacket would have made sense in Pescadores. Bilbao was a land of reds and grays.

"Churches, señor?" the guide mumbled. "Churches, señor?"

And Frog knew that this was Bibo's contact.

"What would you suggest?"

"The Cathedral de Santiago, señor. It's across the river, señor, in the Casco Viejo. You can approach it through the Siete Calles."

"Ah, the Seven Sisters." Frog had familiarized himself with local lore. He couldn't bump in a strange town and not have his own little book of knowledge. Siete Calles was the medieval part of Bilbao. All Seven Sisters ran to the riverbank like the ribs of some dead giant. That's what the Basques liked to think. The giant would rouse himself when the Basques were ready to revolt. And the seven ribs would ride on a sea of blood.

"It's a true Gothic cathedral, señor. It will give you much pleasure. But you must be careful of the viejos who sleep outside the church. They are foreigners, señor. And they have scissors in their pants. They will cut your pockets off if you get too close."

"I'll remember that," Frog said, and walked out of the Carlton. He was in no hurry to meet the boy general. He went up to the Jardines de Albia, where old men in black berets occupied most of the benches. The hats were like black pies on their heads. The Basques had gone to war in such berets. And Holden wondered if all the old men were anarchists.

He crossed the river at the Puerto del Arenal, above the Siete Calles, and entered the old medieval town. He could catch the reflection of buildings in the muddy brown water. He walked on the Calle Sombrerería. Hatmakers Street. There were images of the Virgin with a crown on Her head in almost every window. The Queen of Bilbao. One or two men were following Frog.

He ducked into the cathedral. It was cool inside the door. The Virgin of Santiago was also wearing a crown. Women prayed near the altar. Frog didn't find one man in the cathedral.

He went outside on the Carrera Santiago. The outer walls of the cathedral looked like they could float. It was under this curious shelter that Frog discovered the viejos, bums who lived here without a blanket.

Frog didn't draw his gun. He recognized Bibo right away. The boy general had hid the scar on his face with a torn handkerchief. Frog could have shot him through the head.

"Bibo, you shouldn't have tried to kill the old man like that . . . his restaurant is sacred ground."

"And I suppose he's been an angel with me, eh, El Presidente? I had to move out of Pescadores. He sent his killers. They frightened all my cows. But he has no authority in Bilbao . . . and I wouldn't touch that splendid pistol in your waistband. It's a booby trap. Did you think you could have a gun smuggled into my airport and not pay the fee?"

"I paid enough for that gun, Bibo."

"But the smuggler is dead."

"What if I didn't believe you? I have my own underground, General. It's never failed me before. And I've been to some hairy places."

"But not Bilbao. You're welcome to pull the trigger. But I should tell you, Presidente. You found the gun under a three-legged chair. It was wrapped in silver. It has a very long nose."

"Bibo, what the hell is this fight about?"

"Please sit. A caballero who stands too long in one spot always arouses suspicion."

And so Frog crouched among the viejos, under the flying walls of the cathedral.

"I was Howard's spy. He discovered me in Santander. I was twelve years old and starving. Howard took me in. Not to stroke or kiss. He dangled me in front of rich merchants. He brought me along when he had to bargain with a maricón. We were in Berlin many, many times. I carried papers for Howard. And when our war began, he financed an army for me. I was one more piece of Howard's puzzle. The jigsaw general."

"You still kept Franco out of Pescadores."

Bibo laughed inside his throat. The handkerchief dropped from his face. He looked like some scorched lantern.

"Holden, it was Howard's idea. Howard kept the Fascists away from Pescadores as long as he could. I betrayed none of my men. I rode into battle on a horse. I was a ferocious warrior. I earned all my scars. But I was inside a little box . . . I formed other alliances. And Howard didn't like it."

"But you had him in your palace. You could have finished him off."

"Howard wouldn't have come to Pescadores all alone. He brought you."

"Bibo, I'm just another bumper. I'm last year's news."

"Don't ridicule your talents. I was thinking of a soldier . . ."

"I wasn't a soldier. I have flat feet."

"This soldier arrived in Pescadores in 'forty-six. He was carrying a money bag for Howard. The whole town fell in love with him. He was very shy. Even my cows worshiped him."

"If it's my dad, I don't want to hear about it."

"He'd come to kill me. That was his mission. But somehow he couldn't. Or he didn't want to. He was a complex man. 'Watch out for Phippsy,' he said. 'General, don't turn your back on him.' And I never saw him again. So how could I have butchered his son?"

"You shouldn't be that sentimental, Bibo. If he'd bumped you, he might not have taken it out on himself. And he would have been kinder to Mrs. Howard."

"Yes, Mrs. Howard. The negrita he never married. I know your past, Presidente. I memorized it."

Frog was one more viejo under that curious wall. "Soon you'll ask me to share some paella with you."

"The Basques have banished paella. We would have to go to one of the forbidden restaurants behind the Plaza Nueva, where only imbeciles and the very rich eat."

"What about tourists like me?"

"Bilbao doesn't encourage tourists. There are bombings twice a month. And you're a businessman passing through a town without many strangers."

"You have to promise not to hurt Phippsy . . . or I can never leave. If I get you your bonds, will that be enough?"

"The bonds and a million a month. I will have to nurse my cows after what the viejo has done."

"General, I'm sorry. The cows might have to suffer."

But before Holden could finish, a face was upon him. It was the broommaker, Kit Shea . . . and a comrade from the Westies. They had pistols inside their hats, which they held belly high.

"Jesus, Kit, will you get out of here while you have your arms and legs? Go back to the Copenhagen."

"No more closets," Kit said.

"How did you find me?"

"You're losing your touch. I trailed you right to JFK. That wouldn't have happened a year ago. You always book five or six flights. But I followed you, Holden, door to door."

"Who's that?" Holden asked about the other man, who was as thin and wiry as Shea.

"No questions. Now ease yourself. Slowly, slowly. So I can have a better look."

"Does Phippsy know you're here in Bilbao?"

"He doesn't have to know. I'm on retainer. Me and my friend."

Holden crouched in front of the boy general, who wouldn't blink or acknowledge the two Westies. And Holden had a bumper's melancholy. He didn't know how to keep Bibo *and* Kit from dying, and he didn't want to choose. Kit had been a loyal rat. And Bibo's history had gone back to Holden Sr. Frog began to feel more and more like the shell of his dad. He could see little men with strangling wires approach the cathedral walls.

"I'm not giving up Bibo, Kit. You'll have to take me. I won't move."

"You'll move," Kit said, and Frog could recognize the classic Westie. The thought of murder made Kitty's eyes dance. "I always loved to splinter kneecaps."

"Phippsy might not appreciate that."

"Yeah, I worked for him when you were in diapers. You're his chauffeur, that's all. Like your dad."

The little men stood behind the Westies with their wires. And Holden was at some zero hour.

"General," he whispered. "I need them alive." He wasn't sure whether Bibo had signaled to the little stranglers, who put their wires away and knocked both Westies to the ground, took their pistols and their hats.

And Kit Shea, who'd survived Sing Sing and the Tombs and the worst waterfront wars, lost that quickness in his eyes. "Holden, where am I?"

"You're with me, Kit."

He collected the two Westies and marched them out of the Casco Viejo, leaving the Calle Sombrerería to stranglers and other murderous old men.

18

He'd been a nursemaid in Bilbao, nothing more. He'd had a conversation with Bibo outside a cathedral. He'd rescued a pair of bumpers who were older than himself. Bilbao had defeated him. Its snaking river, its black-pie hats, its parks and streets that were anarchist hunting grounds. He'd solved Paris and Rome. He'd danced along the Tiber, read all the riddles in the walls of Notre Dame, but the language of Bilbao looked like children's Greek. He couldn't read all those crazy letters in a row. Mintegitxueta. Erakustazoka. Santutxu. Solokoetxe. Ibaizábal.

He returned to Esterhazy. Howard wasn't in the dorm. Not even the president of Hester Street Hungarian could help the Frog.

"Morton, I was counting on you. He was your favorite cantor."

"Not my favorite," Morton said. "He turned our home into a factory. He built shelves for us. It was like a bribe. He made himself our captain. That's how it is with billionaires. They're always taking over. He had a fax machine near his bed. He was buying and selling on his personal phone. His hoodlums ran in and out. We became part of his circus . . . and I couldn't forget Kronstadt. I'll never forgive the great Hirsch."

"But if he was so comfortable here, what happened?"

"He got a phone call. His head turned blue . . . he abandoned all his friends. It was cozy while it lasted. But Hirsch didn't need us anymore. He wrote us a check and disappeared from our lives."

"People have been trying to kill him."

"That's no excuse," Morton said. "A captain has to be nice to his men."

$$\mathbb{X}$$

Frog journeyed up to the Phipps Foundation in three separate cabs. It was a habit he couldn't break. He had his own infernal geography. He had to double the distance, no matter what the destination. There were uniformed guards inside the foundation. Holden had to sing like a cantor to get upstairs.

Phipps' office was crowded with all kinds of sheriffs. The billionaire sat behind his desk in that old green cardigan of his. He was whispering to Paul Abruzzi. Then he looked up at Holden with his watery eyes.

"Where were you, Sid?"

"In Bilbao."

"That's a laugh. I'm falling apart and my number one man has gone on an excursion into Basque country. You should have been more considerate. What were you doing in Bilbao?"

"I had a talk with Bibo."

The billionaire started to cackle. The cackling turned into a cough. He clutched Paul Abruzzi's sleeve. "Did you hear that, Paul? He's as dumb as his own saintly dad. . . . Sid, while you were sightseeing in Bilbao, Bibo snatched my little girl."

"Judith?"

"What other little girl do I have? He got you out of the way and had a free hand."

"It was my idea to meet with him."

"Volunteered yourself, eh?"

"Yes, I was bargaining . . . to end your battles."

"And what sort of bargain did you strike?"

"He wants his bonds and a million a month."

The billionaire was cackling again. He coughed so hard, Paul Abruzzi had to reach inside his cardigan and stroke the knobs of his back.

"Sid, you are dumb. You really are. . . . The bonds are mine, and Bibo knew he couldn't get a million out of me. He was stalling, playing for time, while his shitty little anarchists grabbed my girl."

"Suppose it wasn't Bibo."

"Go on, tell him, Paul. Educate the imbecile."

"A certain Mr. Bronshtein got in touch after we discovered that Howard's daughter was missing."

"Solomon Bronshtein," Phipps said to the Frog. "Your partner in crime. You sold him Aladdin's goods while he was plotting against me."

"And what did Bronshtein say?"

"He didn't have to say very much, Sid. 'Mrs. Vanderwelle.' And then he hung up. But Paul will bring her back, won't you, Paul?"

"I'll deliver her myself. I promise."

"And where is she?" Frog asked.

"Some warehouse, I imagine. In the South Bronx."

"Or a bungalow in Queens."

"What's he babbling about?" the billionaire asked, his eyes like two ferocious animals.

"It's nothing, Howard. Holden rescued my daughter-in-law from three crazy brothers."

"The Pinzolos," Howard Phipps said. "Rat and Red Mike. I wouldn't forget Holden's biggest gambit. But why's he interfering?"

"He wants to muddy the waters, Howard. That's all. I have my leads. Bronshtein is a novice in New York."

"But novices often do unexpected things," Holden said, walking away from Howard's sheriffs.

"Where are you going, Sid? Paul might need you in his investigations."

"I'll do better on my own."

"You work for me," the billionaire said. "I'll decide. You draw on my bread and butter."

"Then I'll stop drawing. Good-bye."

And suddenly all that truculence was gone. "I'm helpless without you, Sid. You're like family."

"No I'm not. I'm just the imbecile you hired in place of my dad. One more Holden in your treasure chest."

"I could prevent you from leaving, Sid. I have guards everywhere. They could pull down your pants and spank you. All it takes is a word from me."

"Howard," Paul said. "I—"

"Shut up. I'm talking to Sid."

"Let them try to spank me, mister."

And Holden fled.

None of the guards tampered with him. He took his

usual lopsided routes, north to south and north again, and landed at the Manhattan Mimes. Judith Church wasn't savage with him. She sat in her loft without the mummers. She wore a dark body stocking. She was like some phantom in black, with gray, gray hair. Her knees formed a perfect line.

Holden kneeled next to her. "Mrs. Church, I want to find Judith. But I'm in the dark. Help me."

Holden gripped her hand. "Help me."

"She's already dead, isn't she, Frog?"

"Not if she's part of this insane struggle. There's nothing to bargain with unless she's alive. But I can't hold all the pieces in my head. Help me. I have to know. Why did you work for Howard after all he did?"

"I started the Mimes on my own. I think every unemployed actor in New York must have auditioned for me. I didn't know it then, but Howard brought them up to Vermont on a special bus. It gave me a feeling of power . . . to pick and choose. And to have a team of actors without words. Because I had stopped speaking at Elsinore. We trained very hard. It was all so serious. And then we began to speak, like children in a fable. I had to discover every word all over again. That's what got me out of Elsinore. The Mimes. Howard watched us perform somewhere. He knew I despised him, but he sent an emissary, a sweet man."

Frog moaned to himself. "Howard sent my dad to you."

"Yes. Micklejohn. He came with a proposition from Howard to put on little events . . . for a handsome price. It was fun at first. We were only swindling other swindlers."

"And every time Howard needed something, he sent my dad."

"Yes. Nothing could have been accomplished without your father. He was the go-between. He was the glue. He argued for Howard. He was an eloquent man."

"That's funny. My dad never said a word to me."

Frog recalled those long, terrible silences between them. He couldn't bear to think about his dad.

"Tell me, Mrs. Church, is Judith Howard's daughter?"

"Yes."

"And you invented that fable of other men."

"To hurt Howard. His minions would never have dared sleep with me. They were frightened of his every move. And I wasn't sane enough to seduce the local woodcutter. . . . Howard would come up to Elsinore, blindfold me, and make love to a madwoman."

"And you bit him on the mouth."

"I clawed his eyes. I left scars on his back. He has arthritis from the wounds I made. It's been like that ever since we met. I run from Howard. He chases me. He's cruel. I punish him. He couldn't buy me with his Supper Club or the Manhattan Mimes. And I took away his own daughter. Now he loves her twice as much. That's why she was stolen. I'm sure of it. Howard will have to surrender . . . if it's not too late."

"She's alive, Mrs. Church. Trust me. I've been in my own battles."

"And you'll bring her back?"

"I'll try," Holden said.

Kronstadt was some kind of key. He felt it in his bones. That uptown heiress would lead him to little Judith. Frog only had to follow her tracks. It didn't matter that

Kronstadt wasn't in the neighborhood. Frog knew how to deal with the dead.

"Mrs. Church, tell me about Marcus Reims."

"Marcus Reims was a fiction, one of Howard's invented names."

"Did he ever use it at the Supper Club?"

"He didn't have to. He'd changed hats. He was Howard Phipps."

"And did he talk of Frieda Kronstadt?"

"Of course not. He'd killed her. He wouldn't mention Kronstadt to me."

"And Reims was her partner?"

"And her pimp."

"But they did have other partners?"

"Hundreds. Howard was very enterprising."

"But think, Mrs. Church. Did you hear a name?"

"Do you know how hard we had to dig? It took us years to locate Morton Katz. And there could have been other Kronstadts. Howard was very efficient at burying his past."

"Did you stumble onto some gang . . . like the Westies?"

"Mr. Holden, we weren't looking for gangs. . . . I want my child. I can lend you the Mimes. They've been searching for Bronshtein. I think he's in France."

"No. Bronshtein wouldn't return to his nest. Howard could pick him off."

"Then where is he?"

"Squirreled away . . . with your daughter."

"Mr. Holden," she said, her hand still in his. "We can mount whatever installation you wish."

"Installations won't get me to that furrier or little

Judith. I don't need fables . . . like that afternoon in Queens when I met Dr. Garden, and all the Mimes were in masquerade. That wasn't you I saw, pretending to be Fay."

"No."

"I'm glad," Holden said. "It always bothered me. I mean, you're a wonderful actress. But I would have known. Fay is Fay. You borrowed her from Abruzzi, didn't you?"

"Yes."

"And you were coaching her from behind a curtain. You got her to play herself."

His bumper's instincts hadn't failed him.

Big Judith started to cry. Ah, she *was* as beautiful as his dad's black mistress, this dark lady of Elsinore, who'd borne a child in the middle of a forest. And Holden started thinking of woods. Paul Abruzzi was caught in his own maze. He loved Manhattan too much. That was disastrous for a Queens D.A. Little Judith wasn't in any of the five boroughs. Holden would bet his life on that, though it wasn't worth very much. He was the president of a laundering operation called Aladdin, a retired bumper who was good at writing checks. The money in Aladdin's account was almost as lyrical as the great Hirsch. Liquid gold.

He'd had his network of rats, but no rat could help him now. He could have gone to that encyclopedist, Tosh, and gathered up lists of gangs that might have surrounded the mythical Marcus Reims, but he didn't want encyclopedias. Some kind of crazy string had been pulling Holden all along. He'd been lied to, cozened, duped, hurled down flights of stairs, swindled out of his darling, but he was like a sleepwalker on his way to Mrs. Vanderwelle. He unearthed a .22 long from his bedroom-office. He didn't trust package men anymore. He rented a Plymouth, signed for it as S. Holden. He was sick of aliases. And he wasn't going to turn his life into one long installation.

Frog was on a dream ride. He stopped in New Haven, but he didn't have lunch at Phippsy's Italian restaurant, because the waiters might have recognized him and Frog wasn't sure whose side they were on. He bought a hundred pounds of steak and went to Woods Hole, where he took the ferry. He sat inside the carwell with his treasure of meat and arrived on Martha's Vineyard in a thick black fog that obscured the ferry slip. He couldn't see a face. If there was a shotgun party waiting for Frog, he would have broken through in his Plymouth. He had the luck of a sleepwalker.

He crossed over to Chappaquiddick on the little open ferry. The water seemed to boil under Holden. The fog began to lift. He could see the ferryman's face. The smile was enormous, as if the ferryman had been expecting Frog. He wore an orange bib that looked like a bolt of dried blood. Holden couldn't take a chance. When he reached the other side of the channel, he got out of his car and socked the ferryman in the head. The ferryman had the startled look of a baby as he sank into Holden's arms. Holden locked him in the trunk.

He drove to the Cardinales' junkyard and took out the meat. The same pack of dogs appeared. They had blood in their eyes. None of them barked. Holden could have poisoned the steaks. But it would have distressed him to watch so many dogs writhing on the ground. He tossed the steaks into the air, one after the other, and the dogs leapt up as fast as they could, their fat bodies wobbling for a moment. It tormented them that they couldn't catch all the steaks. They looked like rats with big ears. Holden was the candy man. The dogs started to grovel near his legs. They couldn't decide whether to eat the steaks or lick Holden's hand. He didn't want them in that kind of frenzy. He kneeled with them for a while. He scratched their necks. He was the candy man.

Soon they ignored him and gobbled the meat. Holden got up and went toward Ethan Coleridge's orange house. It was Rockaway all over again. Now he was rescuing a new darling. He could never retire.

Minot, Ethan's youngest boy, who had to be in his mid seventies, emerged from behind an ancient toilet commode. Frog was astounded by his quickness. Minot was holding a shotgun that seemed like a toy in his gigantic paws. It was a bumper's paradise on Chappaquiddick. Holden was the amateur here.

"You shouldn't have come, little Sid. This is our island."

"Minot, how's your dad and your brother Paul?"

"Don't distract me. I never bothered you off-island. We left you and Phippsy alone."

Holden shot him between the eyes. Minot collapsed with spittle in his mouth and died without giving up his gun. But Holden had advertised himself with a pop that echoed off toilet commodes and rusted weather vanes and traveled like some swollen arc across the fields and slapped the orange house with an incredible din.

Holden hiked toward the house and Paul came rushing out to greet him like some lovesick cavalier. He had nothing but a shovel in his hands. Holden had to admire his crazy courage.

"You took my brother, didn't you? I told him to wait in the house."

"Paul, give me that shovel."

"What's the point? Minot is dead. I have no one to steal dollars from. Dad doesn't count."

Paul bled enormous teardrops. Holden might have mourned with him, but the shovel was a little too near. He left a perfect little heart in Paul's forehead and then he entered the house.

Ethan was sitting in a chair.

"Ethan, I'm sorry about the boys."

"No, you're not. You're the fucking angel of death. I could see it in your eyes, Sid. I knew the boys would never survive your presence . . . now I can get married again. I ought to kiss your hand. Phippsy cursed us when he brought you here."

Frog had to use all his cleverness against the old man or he might not recover little Judith.

"Tell me about Marcus Reims."

"Don't bother me. I'm grieving."

"I want to know about Marcus."

"A pimp like any pimp, Marcus was."

"And Kronstadt?"

"The society bitch. Phippsy was always falling for blue bloods."

"And you weren't the baron of Rhode Island. Ethan Coleridge hadn't even been born. Who were you?"

"Ettore Cardinale."

"And you brought Hirschele Feldstein into your little crew."

"He was a catch. A cantor who liked to steal. I groomed him. I taught him his trade. And sonny, I was proud when I heard him sing. I paid the highest price for seats at his shul."

"Did Kronstadt get between you and Hirsch?"

"She fancied rough men. She liked to smell my stockings. I let her live on the street. I beat her, Sid, hard as I could. She always wanted more. And then Phippsy spotted her. Jesus, he bent down and washed her feet. He bought her flowers and clothes. He shared his wallet with her. Made her our fucking partner. I had to shell out hard cash."

"And then what happened?"

"Phippsy got into trouble. He lost his slot as a big-time cantor. He could have stayed with us. But he was searching for a synagogue that would have him. Then he left us flat. Moved out West. Joined the Pinkertons."

"Why did he leave Kronstadt with you?"

"I dunno. Maybe he forgot to take her."

"And Marcus Reims was the name he used while he was with your gang."

"Don't you get it? Anybody who wanted to live without a name was Marcus Reims. I was Marcus for a while. So was Phippsy. And a hundred other men. The gang we had was the Marcus Reims. No one could identify us, pin us to a spot . . .'Oh him, he's Marcus, Marcus Reims.'"

"And who killed Kronstadt?"

"Some no-name. Some Marcus Reims. While Phippsy was away in Seattle. Sid, I had to run."

"And you became Ethan Coleridge."

"That was later, much later."

"And Phippsy returned to Manhattan, found this Marcus, and finished him."

"I wasn't there, but that's what I'm told."

"Now tell me where you're hiding his girl."

"His girl is dead. Kronstadt, I mean."

"I want little Judith. Is she upstairs?"

Ethan didn't answer, and Holden started to climb.

"Sidney boy, I'll have to shoot your eyes out if you take another step."

"I'm not Sidney," Holden said. "I'm Marcus Reims tonight."

Ethan gripped one of his family specials, a long-nosed Webley that had been fashionable before World War II. His hand never wavered.

"Ethan, it's a small house. The bullet will ricochet off the walls and you'll injure yourself."

"Sid, I'm sworn to hide that girl. If you mean to go upstairs, then kill me, and there'll be no more Cardinales. You took my sons. Take me."

"I can't."

And Holden continued to climb. He visited the boys' bedroom. It saddened him. They'd accumulated so little in their seventy-five years. Paul had a fishing rod. Minot had a stamp album with a hundred empty pages. Holden found nothing else on their floor.

He climbed up to the attic.

He heard a whimper. He removed a painter's cloth from a heap of old furniture. He found Solomon Bronshtein lying in a little nest.

"Where's Judith?" Holden said. "Bronshtein, I'll ask you once."

The furrier pointed to another cloth. Judith lay under the cloth like a series of broken sticks. Her lips were raw. Her arms had purple bruises. Her cheeks were tiny blue hills.

"Whose work is that?"

"Minot's. He didn't like women in the house."

"Bronshtein, where are your babysitters? And if you lie to me, I'll hurt you more than you can ever dream."

"They're gone. Ethan wouldn't tolerate them. He called them pig people. . . . I think they're in Bilbao."

"Bronshtein, get me some fucking hot water and a towel. And make it quick . . . it's indecent. One of the richest furriers in the world hiding under a drop cloth."

"Holden . . ."

"Get me some water."

Bronshtein scampered around Frog and returned with a basin of hot water and two towels.

Frog had folded his jacket under Judith's head. He wet the towels and patted her face. Her eyes opened.

"Don't talk," he said. "Do you recognize me? Just nod."

"Holden," she said.

19

He called Mrs. Church from Ethan's phone. "Yes, I found her. She'll be fine. . . . I can't tell you where I am. And don't breathe a word to Howard."

Then he activated the little network he still hadn't lost. It was as archaic as drummers from some unremembered war, but a doctor arrived in half an hour. His name was Figs. He'd been Frank Costello's family surgeon. He was living in retirement on the Vineyard. And Holden had to ferry him across the channel.

"What happened to Al?" Figs asked.

"He's sleeping in the trunk of my car."

"That's no good. The police will come."

And Figs found another ferryman.

Figs could have been eighty, but he had the touch of a surgeon. He carried Judith down from the attic in his own arms. Holden found a cot. Figs undressed her, felt every bruise, applied a cream to her face. He prepared beef tea, gave her a sedative, and kicked everybody out of the room.

"She has a slight fever. But it will pass. I wouldn't move her, Mr. Holden. She's pretty banged up. Nothing broken, far as I can tell. We'll have some X rays done. I'll bring my own man. Hospitals can get awful nosy. . . . I'll look in again tomorrow. But let her sleep."

"How much do I owe you, Figs?"

"Not a dime. Your dad did me a favor a long time ago. Otherwise I wouldn't have come. I'm not in the business anymore."

Frog couldn't even get a doctor without his father's ghost.

Figs drank a glass of schnapps with Ethan and disappeared from the orange house.

"Ethan, how did you and your sons get involved in this mess?"

"Bronshtein gave us a million."

"You could never spend all the money you have. It costs you nothing to live in this barren place. You don't even have a goddamn tomato in the house."

"Cash is cash," Ethan said. "And Phippsy shouldn't have been an Indian giver."

"But I thought you were holding his money."

"I got used to having it around. I'm not his personal banker. He could have left the money here. It was safe with us."

"And for that you kidnap his daughter?"

"We didn't kidnap anybody's daughter. We provided lodging, that's all."

"And you let Minot slap her around. You're supposed to be gallant."

"I can't control those boys. I never could."

"I ought to smash your face."

"I wouldn't stop you," Ethan said.

But Frog went upstairs to Bronshtein, who was camping out in Minot's room. The furrier had nothing better to do than appraise Minot's stamp collection.

"It's worthless. He's been collecting thirty, forty years, and the whole album couldn't bring him a hundred-dollar bill. Think of all that wasted effort."

"Bronshtein, he had his millions. Maybe he was looking for a little fun. . . . Why did you bring her to Chappaquiddick?"

"It was Bibo's idea. He figured Ethan would help us. He knew all the enemies Howard had made."

"And did you really think Howard would let you get away with it?"

"Holden, we had no choice."

"You did have a choice. Go for Howard. Not his daughter."

"We tried."

"Ah, I can't believe Schatz is behind this. Bruno wouldn't have come at Phipps with a band of cowboys. Bronshtein, you were meant to fail. The Swisser set you up. And I can't save your skin."

"But you don't have to give me to Howard," Bronshtein said. "I'll write you the fattest check you've ever seen."

"Please," Holden said. "I can write my own checks."

And then there was little Judith. She didn't have the Phipps Foundation or her mama's mimes on Chappaquiddick. Frog couldn't find a single bow among her belongings. He fed her soup and told her not to talk. She could have been his child. He fell in love with her all over again. He couldn't have traded darlings without bumping Minot and Paul. Love sat across the street from a .22 long.

Fay was becoming a shadow in Holden's head. He couldn't seem to love two women at the same time. He wasn't a natural bigamist like Andrushka. He'd love and lose, love and lose. He had no other home than Chappaquiddick. Away from this island he didn't have a chance. He was a child of Chappaquiddick, like Minot and Paul, and Ethan himself. He understood why the Coleridges had come to Chappy. It wasn't to escape the feds. They could have gone to Switzerland with all their cash. But they decided to roost behind a junkyard. And suddenly Paul's fishing rod and Minot's album made sense. They didn't need much company on this side of the channel.

"I love it here," Frog muttered to himself. He'd gotten used to Bronshtein and Ethan and dogs that slobbered near his legs. "I love it here."

"What?"

"You're not supposed to talk."

"Figs told me I'm getting better," Judith announced from her cot.

Frog was terrified. He didn't want her to get away.

"You're not supposed to talk. I'm your doctor when Figs isn't here."

"Then why don't you play doctor and undress me?"

"You're not strong enough," Holden said.

"I want a thorough examination. I demand it."

And he did undress her. He minded all her bruises and kissed her everywhere he could.

And so they had a family together, with Ethan, Bron-shtein, and the dogs. Figs would bring in food from Edgartown. Ethan would often cry in the middle of a meal. "They were good boys. They never deserted their dad." He didn't blame Holden. He stopped calling him the angel of death.

Frog had some remorse about the two boys—he wished Paul hadn't come at him with that shovel—but he was happier than he'd ever been. He was ready to renounce Aladdin and all his check-writing privileges. He'd become a carpenter and earn his keep. He'd have babies with little Judith. But he could feel a stab under his heart, as if his own ribs were telling him something.

He heard the dogs bark, and Holden knew the idyll was over.

Phippsy had arrived on the island with an ambulance and a small platoon. He didn't even say "Hello, Sid." He captured little Judith. She cried and begged, but his sheriffs carted her into the ambulance. Holden could have popped a couple of Sheriffs with his .22. But it wouldn't have gotten Judith back. And Holden under-stood: the old man meant to kill him if he interfered.

It was Ethan who was the bravest of them all.

"Phippsy," he said. "The girl is healing. Why don't you leave her alone?"

"And have her live with cockroaches?" said the bil-lionaire. He didn't have his cardigan. He had a long quilted coat. He turned to the furrier, who'd been silent with Phippsy in the house.

"Come along, Sol. I don't have much time."

The furrier looked at Holden and then he started to run. He reached the next field before the billionaire summoned his sheriffs. Kit Shea was with them. The sheriffs simply marched in the furrier's tracks. They caught up with Bronshtein in that field of toilet bowls.

Frog didn't want to look, but he couldn't take his eyes off that incredible chase. Bronshtein running, running to nowhere. The sheriffs punched him into the ground and delivered their coup de grace: two or three bullets that sounded like the wing-beats of a giant swan.

Phippsy smiled. "How are you, Sid? Care for a ride back to civilization?"

"I think I'll stay here."

Phipps took off in his ambulance, with the sheriffs behind him, and Holden returned to the orange house.

Marcus Reims

20

He had his own sort of stamp album. Frog collected the life of Bessie Wallis Warfield Spencer Simpson (she had as many names as his dad) and her husband, King Edward, demoted to Duke of Windsor because he wouldn't give up the woman he loved. Wallis Simpson was a divorcée. She had a long nose. And she wasn't some great courtesan who could beguile a country. "David," as the king liked to call himself, was the handsome one. He loved to ride horses. Women followed him everywhere. They wanted to marry David. They offered him diamonds and all the hot perfume between their legs. David wasn't interested. He went into permanent exile with Mrs. Simpson. He wandered the world after marrying her in a French château. And for the rest of his life he was a walking fairy tale, the man who had nothing to do. Hitler offered to make him king of the new Nazi England, but he couldn't conquer the Brits. And Holden didn't believe for a second that David would ever have sat on a Nazi throne. The Duke wasn't a turncoat. Frog wouldn't have worn the socks of a traitor king.

David died in 1972. He was buried at Frogmore, on royal grounds, near Windsor, the castle he couldn't have. Wallis became more and more secluded. Her mind began to go. She was "alert only sporadically in her last years," according to the obit Holden collected from the *Times*. He carried pieces about the Duke and Duchess in his wallet.

And the day after Phippsy took Judith from him and had the furrier killed, Frog dreamt he was at an auction in a little grocery store on the island. The auctioneer was a shoe salesman from Edgartown. He had paraphernalia from the Duke and Duchess on display. *His* handkerchiefs, *his* socks, *his* rings. *Her* crepe wedding gown in "Wallis blue," *her* own handerchiefs, the baubles he'd given Wallis, emerald panthers and lions. Holden wouldn't let anyone else bid. He kept writing out blank checks and hurling them at the auctioneer. And when he had no more checks to write, he howled and woke up from his dream.

He went downstairs and had corn flakes with Ethan. There wasn't any milk in the house, and they had to eat the corn flakes dry. Their chewing sounded like little explosions at the end of the earth.

"Ethan, why didn't Phippsy bump you when he had the chance? You harbored Bronshtein. You were holding his girl."

"I was his tutor," Ethan said. "Phippsy wouldn't forget that."

"Come on, he knew all along where Judith was. First I thought it was Dr. Figs, that Figs had told him. But it wasn't Figs. He knew. That's why he let Paul Abruzzi put on a big show. He'd never rely on Abruzzi, not an old Pinkerton like him. He knew exactly where Bronshtein would go. And I was his little arrow. I got there first and did my business. Ethan, you sold out your own fucking boys."

"I did not."

"You did. You let them die. And I'll tell you another thing. You're the Marcus Reims who killed Kronstadt. It had to be you. No one else in the gang would have touched her. You were angry. She'd been your girl. And the cantor didn't take her to Seattle. She was your territory again. . . . What happened, Ethan? Did you hit her a little too hard? Were you drunk?"

"I was as sober as a man eating corn flakes with little Sid."

"I'll bet you were. But Hirsch signed her away when he left her with you. It was like a death warrant."

"You'd make a wonderful lawyer, Sid. I like the way you present a case. I was seething. I demolished a few of my own boys, but it wasn't the same thing. I never loved Kronstadt. She was an uptown tart. But I'm a man of principles. I wanted her back. She wouldn't have me. She only wanted the little gentleman from Milwaukee. That was Hirsch's title. 'The little gentleman.' I followed her home, strangled her, beat her until my arms were all blue. And then I ran from that city of synagogues."

"And Hirsch bumped another Marcus Reims."

"The best boy I had. It was compensation. I mean, the cantor was justified. He had to take from me."

"But he wouldn't kill his own tutor."

"Not over Kronstadt. Phippsy wasn't a fool."

"You ran to Rhode Island and you've had a relation-ship with the cantor ever since."

"Spasmodic, I'd say. Phippsy had his foundation. He met with kings. He couldn't afford to be seen with the Cardinales. But we did piecework for him. Got rid of pests. Minot never liked him. But Minot never liked anybody, not even his dogs."

"And when you got into trouble with the federal prosecutors, it was Howard who fixed it."

"Yes. He was the fixer. We had a house in Chappy. We agreed to disappear. The bargain was that we couldn't step off the island. We had to sit on all the change we had. It was some piece of change. But it calmed the boys, having all this money around. They felt they had a future. And then he comes here with his bumper and starts to bleed us. The boys wanted revenge. We took Bronshtein's million. And Minot beat the daughter, but he didn't go all the way. Not like Kronstadt."

"And you knew Howard would come for her."

"We had to teach him a lesson. He was taking my boys for granted. I couldn't allow that. I'm their papa."

"And where do I fit?"

"Eat your corn flakes," Ethan said.

"What's my future?"

"You don't have one."

"Are you going to pop me while I'm in bed?"

"Me? Never. I'm fond of you, little Sid. But you'll never leave this island. You know too much. You saw Bronshtein suffer. You got close to Bibo in Bilbao. You might make a government witness."

"And if I'd gone into the ambulance with Howard, would that have been the end?"

"No. The daughter was there. He would have delivered you in one piece. But I figure he's left two or three of his henchmen on the island."

"Westies like Kit Shea."

"Yes, Kitty's one of a kind. Always been loyal to Howard."

"Will they come in through the window?"

"No. They'll wait for you outside. I'm still a baron. They wouldn't violate my hearth."

"And you'll help them?" Frog asked.

"I wouldn't lift a pinky for Shea. But you're on your own, little Sid."

"Fair enough," Holden said. He finished his corn flakes and went up to his room in the attic. He could catch the fields of junk from his window . . . and the white sea. He couldn't forget Bronshtein and the futility of his fat feet. Phipps shouldn't have exposed him to that. He cleaned his .22, found Paul's shovel, and strode into the flattened wilderness.

The dogs were in the far field. They wouldn't have been silent with Westies around, unless Kit had drugged them or supplied his own treasure of meat. He couldn't stop thinking of that Duchess who died alone. A crazy song ran inside Holden's head. *I danced with the woman who danced with the man who stole Wallis Simpson's pants.*

He stumbled upon one of the dogs, lying with its belly slit. It was like stepping on a path of bloody stones as Holden followed the trail from dog to dog. Kitty had clubbed them with his famous broom handle and cut their bellies open, so they couldn't bark or crawl to

Sidney Holden. He felt bereaved without Minot's dogs, oddly orphaned.

Then he heard the Westies. Their laughter jumped across the fields like a loud clap. The Westies shouldn't have revealed themselves with Holden in the neighborhood. He followed the invisible cord their laughing made. Kit and his comrade from Bilbao were sitting among the weather vanes, playing poker for pennies.

Holden marched up to them with the shovel in his hands and cracked their skulls. It meant no more to him than a sneeze. He'd become a wild man on Chappaquiddick. Ah, but they shouldn't have taken such pleasure in slaughtering the old furrier. Someone had to sing kaddish for Bronshtein. And there was no other cantor on the island.

But it still puzzled Frog. Kit wasn't a slacker. He'd followed Holden into the heart of Bilbao. He wouldn't have parked himself in a field like that, exposed himself to the elements and Sidney Holden, unless he were waiting for a signal of some kind. It was a pop. Kit was waiting for Ethan's Webley to go off. Ethan was supposed to kill the Frog. And the Westies would come into the house, finish Ethan *and* the corn flakes, and the circle would complete itself. Howard would be home free. No more Ethan, no more Frog, no more Marcus Reims to remember him by.

Frog didn't return to the house. He had no real grievance against the old man. And what more could he discover? He abandoned his car. He didn't know how many more Westies were on the island. And he'd rather they didn't take target practice on a moving Plymouth. He ran across the fields. He loped around a deserted country club because it could have been a haven for Westies. He arrived at the Chappaquiddick ferry. Figs must have let the ferryman out of Frog's trunk. Al stood at the wheel with a hat to hide whatever swelling he had from Frog's sock in the head. The ferryman wasn't alone. He was chatting with two Westies. And Frog didn't feel like a shoot-out on the little green ferry.

He tossed his shovel into the water. He took off his shoes and jumped into the channel. The dark dead water had deceived him. The currents were swift under the unbroken skin. Twenty minutes of furious paddling left him inside the sink. The currents kept pulling him back to the Chappaquiddick shore. Finally Frog got off the island. He managed to swim two hundred feet.

He was the colossus of Martha's Vineyard, a colossus without shoes. He trundled through Edgartown in his bare feet and knocked on Figs' door. Figs seemed uncertain about letting the fugitive in.

"Find someone else, Holden."

"There is no one else."

And Holden crept into the house. Figs gave him a blanket to wear and some woolen socks.

"I knew you'd bring trouble," Figs said. "I told you. I'm out of the business."

"So am I."

"It's that damn bootlegger, Howard Phipps. I've seen it happen before. He's turned on you. You're on his death list."

"Looks like it," Holden said.

"You don't have a Chinaman's chance."

"I'd have to agree."

"He gets dependent on a person, grows to regret it,

and it fills him with rage. . . . Your dad was a little more clever. He kept his distance."

"Dr. Figs, he had a heart attack in a whorehouse and fell down the stairs."

"But it was a natural death."

"Yes and no. Phippsy devoured him, from the inside."

"Holden, what do you intend to do?"

"Hurt the son of a bitch."

21

He felt like a kid in the custody of an old bank robber. Figs gave the orders in Edgartown. Holden sat in the house. He kept thinking of Kronstadt, the woman who was so ambiguous she was barely allowed a first name. Frog imagined her with a long nose, like the Duchess of Windsor. And suddenly he had the shakes. Kronstadt had also died without her duke. She'd gone into a Manhattan of renegades, fell in love with Marcus Reims, the cantor who had a funny idea of religious services.

"Frieda," he said.

"Who's that?"

"Nothing, Doctor. I was just giving some woman a name."

"No one's called Frieda anymore. I haven't met any Friedas in a long time. . . . The old man's gonna kill you. You know that. Once he puts his mind to something, that's it. I have to get you out of here, Holden. You're dangerous company."

"I could leave right now. You've done enough for me."

"You'd be dead in five minutes."

Figs had a network of his own, the remnants of some Mafia that had been bumped out of place, a forgotten family that could be called back into motion by Figs.

Two young men arrived in Salvation Army uniforms, the grandsons of a retired warlord. They had uniforms for Holden and Figs, blue on blue. Holden smiled. It was the nearest he'd ever been to his dad. A soldier of sorts, with black bone buttons and blue epaulets.

The four of them got into a car and drove onto the Vineyard ferry. Holden didn't have a fake mustache. But he had the absent stare of some devotee. He was a zealot in his uniform, a converter of souls. None of Phipps' sheriffs would have made him.

"Holden," Figs said once they were on the mainland. "You ought to try the Far West. I have connections in Vegas. But I'd recommend Oregon. A man can lose himself in the north woods."

"I've been there," Holden said. "The eagles are too big. They could scratch your eyes out. . . . I'm still better off in Manhattan."

"You're just crazy about islands, that's all."

The young men drove him into Manhattan. They let Frog off near the fur district.

"We could find you a pad," Figs said. "All it would take is a phone call."

"You've done enough. I'd write you a check, but I'm not sure it's worth anything."

"Go on," Figs said. "I wouldn't take money from a soldier."

The young men laughed. And Holden edged into the city like an invisible man.

He had a few safe houses, but he couldn't trust them. Anything Frog had ever touched was tainted now. He wasn't forlorn. He'd loved Mrs. Howard. He'd loved the twig. He'd loved Fay. He'd hated his dad and loved him a little. He'd loved his own tailor, who was a spy for Bruno Schatz. He loved the cantor's little girl. He wasn't forlorn. Lots of things could happen to a man who was supposed to die.

He wasn't concerned about shelter. Frog had to get his own feel of the streets. He had to occupy Manhattan again, even if his home was Chappaquiddick. He missed the salt air, the field of toilet bowls, and his dead dogs. He sailed across the city in his usual quota of cabs and arrived at Morton Katz's golden-age club. Two sheriffs were guarding the door. They laughed at Frog in his service cap. "Hey soldier, how's life?"

He went inside the Esterhazy Houses and approached Katz's dorm with some kind of dread. He couldn't locate the little president of Hester Street Hungarian. Katz wasn't in the game room or the community chapel. No one could account for him. And Frog had to wonder if Katz had disappeared for life, one more casualty of the Kronstadt case. . . .

Frog walked to Hester Street and found the little president in his office at the shul.

"Who are you?"

"Sid Holden."

"You're not Holden. You're one of Hirsch's tricksters. And I wouldn't tell you where Holden is even if I knew."

"Morton, look at me."

"You think I'm a dunce? Hirsch has a whole acting studio behind him. He can manufacture faces and coats."

"Look at me."

"I'm looking." And the little president started to cry. "If you are Holden, then please run. Because Hirsch has hoodlums everywhere . . . but what are you doing in such an awful coat?"

"Have they hurt you?"

"Give me a definition of 'hurt.' A man came. He sat down near my bed. Nothing rough. A distinguished man with white hair. Like Walter Pidgeon. He said: 'You never saw Holden. You never met Holden. You never talked to Holden.' And he left. But I recognized him. He's in the papers a lot."

"Paul Abruzzi."

"Yes. The district attorney of Queens. And if such a man is on Hirsch's side, Hirsch can do whatever he wants. That's when I moved into the synagogue. But his voice comes through the walls. I can't forget how sweet it was. He's right. I am his choirboy. I always was. I never recovered from Hirsch. It was like having a terrible knock on the head. What a melodic line! He never dramatized, like the other cantors. He never wore his hair long. He didn't pretend to be some King David. He was Hirsch. His robes were linen, not silk. He hardly had a beard. He was song, pure song, without the coloratura of lesser cantors. Hirsch wouldn't entertain. He pleaded for our lives. He spoke for every sinner in the shul. That's what killed me. A bandit like him had God's ear . . . still does. And we have to crawl like mice. Holden, get out of here."

"But I can't leave you like this. Abruzzi could come again, and he might not be so kind."

"He wouldn't touch me, not in Hirsch's old house. . . . What did you ever do to Hirsch?"

"Does it matter? I'm his enemy now. If there is trouble, Morton, go to Chappaquiddick and wait for me."

"I'm not such a world traveler, Mr. Holden. Between here and Esterhazy, that's what I know."

And Frog walked out of the shul.

He was the invisible man. Not because Phippsy seemed to want him dead, or his own uniform lent him some kind of a cloak. Frog had lost his contact points. He was a pariah with one particular talent. He went to the Algonquin, sat near Abruzzi's Round Table. The invisible man wasn't taking a chance. He hunched in his chair, with his service cap over one eye. He had a gin and tonic, and the waiters were amused to see a Salvation Army soldier guzzle gin. But they forgot the soldier after his second drink. Abruzzi's acolytes began to arrive, detectives who'd become his private enforcers, who would have done anything for Paul. And then Paul appeared with that handsome white hair, the prince of this hotel.

"Children, any word of the brat?"

"Paul, we've checked all his corridors, all his haunts. We've wired up Aladdin—"

"Not so loud," Paul said. "He's flown the coop. That's a fact."

"He wasn't on the ferry. He wasn't on a plane. We would have been down on him like a hawk."

"Well, the old man has given this commission to me. I won't look silly, understand? Holden has to be found."

Paul winked at a waiter and had his first Irish coffee. Then he started to hum and Holden became some trifle he could store in his pocket with petty cash and deposit slips and invitations to dinners he'd never attend. His boy Rex had won the Pulitzer Prize. His daughter-in-law was back with her family. And Paul would become a justice of the State Supreme Court as soon as there was a seat on the bench. He had years and years to go.

Petitioners approached him, the little men of his own county who came into Manhattan to beg personal favors from Paul. "Your Honor," they called him, since he was already like a judge.

"Your Honor, what about that franchise at Cunningham Park?"

"Don't get greedy."

"But we could triple our volume if we had one little nod from Howard Phipps."

"Do you think he would bother with the likes of you? He has his foundation to run."

Paul's bladder began to ache after the fifth Irish coffee. "I ought to go and tinkle . . . mind the store," he said to his acolytes. And he trudged down the little crooked staircase to the Algonquin's toilet, his pockets thick with notes. But he never had the chance to pee. He felt something like a hammer on his head. It was only a fist. Paul dropped to his knees. A hand pushed his face down into the elegant muck of the marble floor.

"Hello, Paul."

"Who is it?"

"Your angel, Sidney Holden."

"I should have figured you'd be in the toilet, waiting

to get the drop on me. That's why you've been so scarce."

"You're wrong, Paul. I've been dogging you day and night. You shouldn't talk about commissions from Howard. That wasn't nice. And I like the way you stuff pieces of paper in your pocket. How are things at Cunningham Park?"

"Holden, what do you want?"

"Can't you guess?"

"You wouldn't kill me. I'm not some barfly. I'm the D.A."

"I have nothing to lose, Paul. I'm already a dead man."

"But I could call off Howard's bloodhounds."

"The hounds are yours."

And Holden pushed a little harder, until Paul's face squeezed against the marble tiles and his mouth kissed the floor. He seemed to talk out of some great hollow. "Holden, Fay's been asking about you."

"Stop it, Paul. She's on another planet."

"But Fay—"

Holden pushed some more. And Abruzzi had the imprint of a tile on his forehead, like some fabulous mark of the Algonquin.

"Paul, does she remember her children?"

"Sometimes."

"And you?"

"Hardly at all."

"Now tell me where little Judith is?"

"I don't know."

Holden pushed and pushed until Paul's mouth started to bleed. He was beginning to strangle on his own blood.

"Where's little Judith?"

"I . . . don't . . . know." Each word Paul uttered cost him more blood. "Howard wouldn't . . . confide . . . in me."

"Yet you'd kill for him. You had your shooflies wire up Aladdin so I'd pull my own trigger when I walked in. You're a sweetheart, Paul. You really are."

Holden could have dispatched him with one more push. But he wanted Paul to come out of the toilet alive, to face his own detectives with dirt on his clothes, the nimble prince of Queens. Frog couldn't linger. A guest of the Algonquin might decide to use the facilities and discover Paul. Frog stepped over the district attorney, washed his hands, and walked out of the Algonquin.

He dialed Mrs. Church from the corner phone booth. He could have gone uptown to the Mimes, but he was sick of running around as God's little soldier. Frog needed some sleep. "It's Holden, Mrs. Church. Is Judith all right?"

"I can't talk," she said. "Where are you?"

"Near Grand Central."

"I'll meet you in half an hour. Under the clock."

And Frog loped toward Grand Central Station. It was after the commuter hour. And the terminal was filled with homeless men and women, nighthawks, and religious soldiers like himself. Frog looked up at the barreled ceiling and caught a glimpse of paradise: all the monsters of the zodiac were nesting in a faint green field. They couldn't frighten the Frog. They were like lyrical children pinned to the sky. Taurus. Cancer. Capricorn. Aries with his horns and beard and big, big, eyes. What if Frog himself were some night sign? The lost brother of Aquarius. Scorpio's cousin. The monsters stared down at him with such warmth that Holden wanted to die. These were the only playmates he'd ever have.

He wouldn't budge when Mrs. Church arrived. He wasn't being cautious. He was dreaming of rams and lions. And then he watched the sheriffs drift into the terminal, one by one, blocking the exits, laughing at the homeless, and looking for Sidney Holden. At first he thought it was some accident that the sheriffs should appear so soon after Mrs. Church. He watched. He waited. The sheriffs buzzed around Mrs. Church. And then he realized that big Judith had managed the whole affair. Frog was in the middle of one more installation. But Mrs. Church hadn't counted on the terminal's peculiar traffic. She couldn't control that much malaise.

Frog drifted past red-faced men with fingerless gloves, starving children, and the sheriffs who clicked their teeth. Mrs. Church stood under the clock. And Frog fell asleep near a little caravan of crates that belonged to the men with fingerless gloves. No one harmed him. And when the cops arrived at curfew, marched down the terminal steps to kick out all the stragglers, anyone without a driver's license or some other proof of address, they didn't disturb him.

"Sorry, soldier," they said as they tore apart the little caravan.

He stayed through the night. He didn't have any stratagems. He woke as the terminal began to fill. A woman removed a sandwich from her attaché case and offered it to him. Frog took the sandwich.

"You must be dreadfully tired," she said, "working through the night, taking care of people. You're the kindest soldier I've ever seen."

And suddenly Frog had his key. He walked to the Phipps Foundaton. He presented himself. The guards at the door wouldn't question a Salvation Army soldier. They must have figured he had an appointment to beg or borrow from one of Phipps' charities. He looked a little lonesome and he could use a shave. But he was harmless under his service cap. He walked through the metal detector the guards themselves had installed. Holden wasn't carrying. He'd lost his .22 while swimming in the Chappaquiddick creek.

He went up to Phipps' office. It was cluttered with shooflies and sheriffs. Frog smiled at the receptionist. He invented a persona for himself, picked it out of the blue.

"I have an appointment with Mrs. Vanderwelle," he said. "I'm Colonel Baxter's aide-de-camp . . . Baxter of the Eastern Territory."

"I'm sorry," the receptionist said. "Mrs. Vanderwelle is ill."

"Then I'd like to see Howard Phipps."

"We never disturb Mr. Phipps while he's having lunch. What's the nature of your appointment?"

"Soup kitchens," Frog said. "Soup kitchens in the Eastern Territory."

"Then I'll direct you to Mr. Atwood. He's handling Mrs. Vanderwelle's affairs . . . third door to the left. His secretary will see you."

And she buzzed Frog into the foundation. He had a kind of merry murder in his blood. He moved toward Phipps' private elevator car. A sheriff stopped him.

"Hey, you with the hat, no one's allowed in that elevator."

Frog socked the sheriff between the eyes and shoved him into a closet. He got into Phippsy's elevator and rode upstairs to the Supper Club. He nodded his head, winked at strangers, and saw Howard having lunch all alone in the middle of that enormous room.

Frog sat down at the next table. Bodyguards, waiters, and the maître d' descended upon him. "Sorry, but we're not open to the public . . . you can't sit here."

"Sure I can," Frog said. "I'm Phippsy's guest."

"Your name, sir?"

"Marcus Reims."

And the old billionaire started to laugh. "It's Holden, can't you tell?"

The waiters drew pistols out of their tight coats. But the billionaire warned them off. "Invite him to my table, Mr. Charles," he said to the maître d'. "And then take a walk. All of you. Scram."

Holden joined the billionaire.

"I recognized you right away. Sid, I never look at coats."

"That's because you have some imagination."

"No. It's the opposite. Markings don't interest me much. Would you care for some curry? I hired a new chef."

"I'll have what you're having."

"You're a growing boy. You can't nibble on crackers and cheese."

"Why not?"

And the billionaire screamed across the length of the Supper Club. "Mr. Charles . . . "

"I don't want another setting, Phippsy. We'll share."

Charles had come running with his cavalry of waiters.

Howard had to dismiss him again. And Holden sat under the murals of that fictitious New York, where each traveler had his own bicycle with wings, and he ate a rat's portion of cheese.

"Go on," Phipps said. "Why don't you strangle me?"

"I don't do mercy killings."

"Mercy killings, huh? You're a regular mortality machine. Do you know how much you cost me this week in damages alone?"

"You can afford it."

"That's not the issue. I'm talking dollars and cents. . . . I've been waiting for you, Sid."

"And wishing me dead."

"It comes to the same thing. I set up a little obstacle course. You passed the test."

"Hirschele, you had my grave prepared on Chappaquiddick. I got lucky, that's all. You made up with the Swisser, didn't you?"

"Had to, Sid. Or he would have run me into the ground."

"Bronshtein was the fall guy. He never had a chance."

"He shouldn't have run around with thieves. The man doomed himself when he kidnapped my daughter."

"Kidnapped? You knew all along she was on the island. That's why you let Paul Abruzzi pish around. Everyone's a player in Phippsy's Supper Club. You were going to arrive with your magic ambulance, rescue Judith, finish off Bronshtein and the whole Cardinale clan."

"You shouldn't have meddled."

"I was trying to save your little girl."

"You shouldn't have meddled. You went to Bilbao. You talked to Bibo. You weren't my Sid."

"Old man, you've had me ticketed for years. I was your sleeper. I killed Red Mike for you. I knocked off the Cuban Maf. And I went into retirement with Fay Abruzzi. But Paul was your man. You took Fay from me, like you took the twig. And then you woke the little sleeper. Why?"

"Had to have some fun, Sid. My birthday was coming up."

Holden couldn't keep his eyes off the murals. Hirsch's dream city began to make sense. The boy cantor had built the twentieth century around himself. All the sky machines and hanging gardens of stone must have "visited" Hirsch while he lived in a coal cellar as the little gentleman from Milwaukee.

"It had nothing to do with birthdays," Holden said. "Or the Manhattan Mimes. Or Aladdin. Or leaky accounts."

"You're right. I wasn't taking early retirement. I'm not like you. I had to flush out Swiss and the boy general, oblige them to make a move."

"What if it was your own paranoia?"

"All the more reason to act. I'm an impatient man."

"So you let me play president of your best laundering operation. That angered Schatz."

"Drove him crazy, Sid. There's a difference."

"And then you took me on the road to the Cardinales, because you figured Schatz might just link up with Ethan and his two children. And you wanted to give Ethan a little shove in Schatz's direction. You hit their pocketbook, demanded three million."

"It was my money. I could draw on whatever I liked."

"But you knew what would happen."

"I was prepared for the consequences, if that's what you mean."

"You didn't wait for Swiss. You started the war. And you sweetened it by taking me to Bibo and asking for your bonds. . . . Old man, you were inches away from dying."

"I'm a gambler, Sid. I gambled on you. I had a whale of a time."

"Where's little Judith?"

"Best not get on the subject of my girl."

"Where is she?"

"Convalescing, Sid. And you can't find her. I didn't raise my girl so she could live with some bumper. Holden, she's not for you."

"You never raised her. She was one more toy."

"Not now," the billionaire said. And Holden was in some kingdom where he couldn't win.

"I suppose you gave Aladdin back to the Swiss."

"Had to. But it doesn't affect your status. You're president for life."

Now it was Holden who laughed. "Every bounty hunter in America wants my blood."

"That can be changed."

"How? If I bump Bibo for you?"

"Bibo's lost most of his ambition. He was only one more anarchist in Bilbao. I let him return to Pescadores. He can't harm me now."

"And Marcus Reims? Marcus is out there, old man. Marcus doesn't forget."

"Don't get silly on me. I'll have to call a doctor . . . or gag you right away."

"Gag me then. Because Marcus wants to know why you abandoned Kronstadt, why you left her in Ethan's hands."

"That Ethan has a big mouth. But Kronstadt's not your business."

"I think she is, old man. We're all Marcus Reims. You. Me. The Coleridges. My dad. Murderers deluxe."

"Shut your mouth, Sid."

"Did you get tired of Frieda? She stopped pleasing the little gentleman from Milwaukee. Got yourself a new kettle of fish?"

The blue-green eyes went pale and watery. The murals surrounding Hirsch no longer mattered. All the luminescence was gone. A bicycle with wings was one more fancy, like piss in a bucket.

"She wouldn't go with me. She had nothing here. Dirty bloomers. The garbage she collected. But she wouldn't go. It was her home, she said."

"But you knew Ethan would kill her."

"Of course I knew."

"Why didn't you kidnap Frieda, knock her over the head?"

"Kidnap Frieda? She'd have bitten off my arm . . . I was helpless. A man without a synagogue. I had to go."

"Did you sing kaddish for her?"

"I was chasing grafters in Seattle. I couldn't run into some strange shul."

"You're a cantor. A cantor can make his own shul. You didn't want to sing for Kronstadt."

"I'd sing for you, Sid. I would."

"Like you sang for my dad. . . . Who gets to bump me, old man? Who gets the nut? Will Abruzzi's men be waiting for me outside the elevator?"

"Don't get morbid. I could learn to forgive and forget."

"I wouldn't let you, old man. I'm going to find little Judith."

Hirschele's eyes recaptured that heartless blue. He was the paradise man, not Sidney Holden.

"You're God's elect," Holden said. "Hirschele, how did you make a whole congregation cry?"

"You weren't there, Sid."

"I talked to the president of Hester Street."

"He was just a choirboy."

"And a witness to the holy man who had people killed."

"Shut your mouth."

"How did you do it? How did you make them cry?"

"Me? I was a crooner, Sid. I had the tonsils. I'd look up at the balcony, see all the lovely daughters, widows, and wives, and my heart was going like mad. That's how come my voice was so sweet. But what would you know? You worship the Duke of Windsor. You wear his clothes."

"Leave the Duke out of this."

"The Duke and his Duchess. Both of them were mad about Hitler."

"Who says?"

"Kiddo, I did an awful lot of deals with the Third Reich."

"As Hirschele Feldstein or Howard Phipps?"

"Both. A cantor's millions were as good as gold. . . . I cheated them out of whatever I could. Guns, art, or blood. I'm a trader, Sid. I dealt with whoever there was to deal. I'm not ashamed of it. But the Duke was Hitler's pal. The Duchess danced with a swastika around her neck."

And for a moment Frog had the desire to throttle Hirschele in his Supper Club. It wasn't the bodyguards that compelled him to wait. Holden wouldn't kill a cantor.

"You're a liar, old man. I have a record of every jewel she ever had. There's no swastika on that list. . . . how much did you pay Mrs. Church to finger me at Grand Central Station?"

"We were talking about the Duchess."

"Come on, did she do it out of loyalty or love?"

"I'm holding the girl, Sid. She had to do what I say . . . or she'll never see her."

"Suicide poker, that's what you like to play. With my dad, with Swiss, with your own little girl. Did Ethan teach you all the rules?"

"There are no rules. That's the beauty of it."

And Frog saw a figure among the other figures. She wasn't a wax doll, like the maître d'. It was big Judith in a party dress she might have worn years and years ago. She looked like a panther. And Holden understood. She belonged in the room. The Supper Club was a graveyard without big Judith. The murals had no melody without her. Hirsch had built himself a crazy shul. The first installation. And Kronstadt must have prepared the way. With her wildness and her dirty feet.

Shit, Holden said. Another Kronstadt. The wild girl of the Supper Club. And Holden could dream of what it had been like. With a full orchestra. Muted trombones.

Dark ladies in dark dresses. With men who were nothing
more than chaperones, in their ties and tails. Big Judith
taking her panther steps, while all the men went out of
their minds. She was there to drive them berserk. And
Hirschele must have seen it as punishment, a visitation
from Kronstadt's secret sister. Not an uptown heiress.
Not a runaway girl. But someone he could never really
control.

Holden was scared. He had to get the hell out of there.
He'd been surfacing around too many ghosts. He got up
from the table and ran out of the club.

22

A wind might have been pulling at him. He walked to Aladdin. He was no longer the invisible man. All of Hirsch's sheriffs knew about this Salvation Army soldier. But Frog wouldn't give up his coat. He wanted to see how Abruzzi's men had triggered his own door. He rode upstairs, expecting a haunted house. He discovered a small hotel. The shop was packed with nailers and cutters, Nick Tiel's old gang. The cutters worked at a furious pace. Frog went to the designer's room. He found the Swiss, who had Nick Tiel's paper tacked to the walls. Andrushka was modeling one of the Swisser's new line of coats, a glorious sable. She'd started as a mannequin in this same shop. She'd thickened a bit during her Paris years. But she was still the girl he'd married.

"Holden," Schatz said. "We've been expecting you. Will you take off that ridiculous coat? I need you around. All the buyers want to meet Sidney Holden."

"Bruno, haven't you heard? I've been sentenced to death."

"Don't be ridiculous. You're part of the corporation. You're president. You sign the checks. Tell him, Andrushka."

"We're counting on you," she said. "We couldn't survive."

"You'll have to." And Holden realized that she'd always been a mannequin, even in the Swisser's arms. Swiss must have lent her out to Bibo and how many other boy generals? Holden's error was that he'd tried to reform the twig, take her out of the fur shop, so she could study Caravaggio. It had been nothing more than cotton candy.

He went into his office. The district attorney's men must have unsprung their trap. Holden looked at the coats he had, the shoes, the ties, the shirts with royal labels. He locked the office and disappeared from Aladdin.

He visited Vermont in his Siberian coat. Farmers stared at him. They'd never seen a Salvation Army soldier. They spoke some kind of patois that Frog couldn't seem to penetrate. "Elsinore," he muttered. "A hospital, a home in the woods." They laughed.

"A hospital. Pas des homes in the woods. Pas ici."

And Frog traveled from Middlebury to Montpelier. He bribed the selectmen of one little town, offered them a donation to fix the local waterfall if they could find Elsinore. The selectmen drove him around to different spots. He entered sanitariums where the boarders had such white faces that Frog couldn't be certain they were alive. He stumbled upon abandoned whiskey stills, the rotten palaces of neglected robber barons. He searched the back rooms of orphanages, where he found old ladies who'd lost their minds, but no one who resembled little Judith. Frog paid for the waterfall. And then he tracked on his own.

He had no more rats to rely on. He couldn't go back into the belly of Manhattan and build a new network of spies. He went deeper into the mountains. It started to snow. He'd rent a car and return it, rent a car and return it, always with the idea that Elsinore was behind the next snowdrift. He began to hear voices in the howling weather. He caught a chill. He had to stop at a country inn and lie under a thick blanket. Frog had a fever. The snow collected outside his window. There was no mud or oil on the ground. He'd arrived at some crystalline world. He wondered if that was Elsinore. He went out dancing in the middle of a storm. He could feel the outline of a building that moved with the snow. But he could never get close enough. The innkeeper had to drag him upstairs to his room. "I used to bump for a living," Frog said. "No one puts his hands on me."

The innkeeper fed him barley soup. When Frog woke, the fever was gone. The innkeeper didn't want to accept money from a Salvation Army soldier.

"I never freeload," Frog said. "I'm a paying guest." He dug into his pocket and took out a little twisted tree of hundred-dollar bills.

"That's too much."

"You've been kind to me."

"What are you looking for, soldier?"

"A house in the woods. Used to be a sanitarium for very rich people."

"Ah, the doctors' place. It's closed."

"Will you take me there?"

The innkeeper lent him some boots. They trudged up a hill. Holden's heart was pounding. They stumbled onto a door in the snow. There wasn't even a proper porch. It was snowing inside the door. Holden realized that the roof was missing. He stepped on a frozen mouse.

He crossed the channel in a rented Plymouth. The ferryman looked him up and down, but he couldn't recognize Frog in his soldier's suit. And Frog didn't have to worry about having Al signal ahead to Ethan Coleridge.

"You some sort of a pilgrim? We don't get a lot of pilgrims on Chappy."

But when he arrived at the orange house, Ethan stood waiting with a shovel. "I'm sworn to kill you."

"Feed me first," Holden said. "I'd like some corn flakes."

They sat at the table, the old, old man with his shovel and Frog. Ethan looked worried. "What if Phippsy changed his plans? I'd be the last to know."

"I keep hearing voices."

"How's that?"

"Voices," Holden said. "I think it's Kronstadt."

"She was always a witch. That's why I choked her. But it's a funny thing. I hear her too . . . every night. It's worse now that the boys are gone. Minot would see the glint in my eye, and he'd say, 'Dada, it's the dead lady.' That softened the blow."

Frog had some corn flakes and closed his eyes.

"You shouldn't nod off in my presence," Ethan said. "I'm holding a shovel on you."

And Frog had his best sleep since he'd gone on the road. He woke in the attic. This hundred-year-old man had put him to bed. Frog was wearing Minot's pajamas. He went downstairs and had his morning dose of corn flakes. There was still no milk in the house. But he found a radish, some raisins, some prunes. He went out into that empire of junk. The toilet bowls were filled with black snow. The weather vanes sat like spears. Holden could have been a gardener in his own garden.

Ethan carried his shovel for two days and then decided to give it up. "I don't have to kill you."

"Do you know where Phippsy's daughter is?"

"Have a radish."

"Do you know where she is?"

"Even if I had a clue, I couldn't tell."

They lived on their meager diet, with millions buried in the house. The ferryman would appear with the most essential rations. He must have been Hirschele's contact. Because Frog never heard the telephone ring.

He tore up his checkbook. He had no desire to haunt the boutiques of Edgartown. But he kept his uniform clean.

Ethan started to panic. He picked up his shovel again. He wouldn't touch the corn flakes.

"I can't chew. Phippsy's coming to get us. He wants my millions. He'll set fire to all my paper, turn it into fuel."

"Aladdin's his fuel. The Swisser has a new line of coats."

"Well, we're sitting ducks. Any fool could rob us."

And when Al arrived in the middle of the night with

two more islanders, carrying empty potato sacks, Holden was there. He sat with Ethan's Webley in his lap.

"Don't try to stop us, pilgrim," Al said.

Frog shot Al in the foot. The ferryman whimpered. "It isn't fair." He left with his two comrades and the potato sacks. But Ethan wasn't satisfied.

"It's not safe. You could steal my treasure. You could get ideas."

"Ethan, I haven't spent a dollar on this island. Go to bed."

One or twice a week Cardinale would attack him with the shovel. Holden's arms were sore from where the shovel fell. But he was fond of this old, old man. He wouldn't hurt Ethan Cardinale. And he still had the blessings of an open field. Winter birds would caw at him, follow him from field to field, but Holden couldn't seem to find much of a trigger for his own life. He'd been bred like some strange plant to bump people. That was the only trigger he ever had. Kronstadt wasn't a witch. She'd lived between the empty spaces, like Holden himself.

His fabric had been the clothes he wore. The stolen designs of David, Duke of Windsor. He was no less of a mannequin than the twig. Now he had no signature. He was a soldier in a junkyard. He shared nothing with Ethan. They never talked. Frog couldn't even remember his own voice.

And then he heard the roar of a minibus. He could see the word MIMES painted on one of the panels. And he wondered if a troupe had come to perform on Chappy. It was his island now. He was standing in a field. The bus swerved around the toilet bowls and stopped in front of

Frog. Mrs. Church got out with little Judith. Judith's face hadn't healed. The mouth was swollen. The bones of her eyes were blue.

"I was never married," she said. "It was all a lie."

"Shh," he told her. "It must hurt to talk."

"There was no Mr. Vanderwelle. I'm not even a lawyer. I never went to school. I lived with mama in the woods."

"Shh," Holden said. He wanted to murder Minot all over again. But Frog had worn Minot's pajamas. He was living in Minot's house. He couldn't even tell the good assassins from the bad.

"I told Mama I wanted to stay . . . stay with you . . . Holden's island."

"Shh," he said.

Big Judith stared down at Frog from that height of hers, a panther without a party dress. She could have swallowed Holden. He was helpless around her, like he'd been with Mrs. Howard. Frog couldn't negotiate with very tall women.

"Holden, I'm lending my daughter to you."

"I'm sick of lendings. I want her to be my wife."

"You're a married man, Mr. Frog."

"Means nothing. I'll get a divorce. . . . Does Howard know you brought her here?"

"He'll get used to it. Give him time. But for God's sake, shut up about marriage. I don't want him to have a stroke."

She kissed her daughter and climbed into the bus. Holden watched her bump across the icy fields. She seemed one more piece of ice in an eternity of ice.

He took little Judith's hand. He led her to the orange

house. Marcus Reims, he muttered. He'd have to bump Ethan. He couldn't keep her around a crazy man. He was shivering. He could see some shadow fly in the window. I'll kill him, Frog said, if he's holding a shovel.

Frog opened the door. Ethan had his shovel. He saw Judith. "The little daughter," he said. His face seemed to flush like a curious rose. He dropped the shovel. "Would you care for some corn flakes?"

Ah, Holden said, I won't have to kill him now.

23

She drove toward the lights of Manhattan in the Mimes'
very own bus, like some mechanic behind the wheel.
Judith didn't own a license. She'd learned to drive at that
madhouse in Vermont. Elsinore, Elsinore, where doctors in blue gowns sat with her while she bumped across
the grounds, the madwoman who belonged to Mr.
Phipps. Steering that wheel was like discovering another language. Almost as good as sex.

Judith's first car was an old Cadillac in the woods that
also served as Elsinore's ambulance. She remembered
all the turns as she went round and round the porches
and kept seeing the same metal rooster that must have
been a weathercock. The rooster made winter noises,
like the cackle of ice.

She returned to Manhattan, parked the bus, showered
at her loft, shaved her legs, searched through her closets.
Judith dressed to kill. A sixty-seven-year-old moll, having to seduce Howard one more time. It wasn't even
noon. She smoked a cigarette, rinsed her mouth with a

shot of rye. "The Supper Club," she said. "The Supper Club."

She put on her coat with the rabbit-skin collar, caught a gypsy cab, and arrived at the foundation like a lonesome mama. Howard's doormen pampered her. "Hello, Mrs. Church." She had her own bodyguard to take her upstairs. She handed the bodyguard her rabbit-skin coat and walked into the restaurant with a pair of naked shoulders.

Howard was at his table. He couldn't take his eyes off Judith. His mouth was shivering. He was like an ancient boy tucked inside a green sweater. "I thought you'd abandoned me. I thought you wouldn't come."

"Didn't I promise you?" she said.

"I thought you wouldn't come."

And Judith stared into the heart of that crazy restaurant, and it was like a jungle that had no end. Her whole life had been defined by the contours of this room, the murals, the ceilings, the walls, the waiters who stood like tin men, the musicians in white pants, hugging their golden horns.

"Come on," she said. "Let's dance."

His face froze against the murals. "I'm a cripple," he said. "I have to wear special shoes."

"You always danced. Even when you were half dead."

He got up from the table, wearing his napkin, and fell into Judith's arms. The orchestra started to wail. It was some lost tune from that time when Howard had his own Cinderella. Judith Church, the dark-eyed belle who danced her days and nights at a palace with polished floors, where the entire population could see down her back.

Howard danced in his heavy shoes. He didn't even
have the courage to look at her. His trombones were
playing "White Cliffs of Dover." Her one romance had
happened in the middle of the war, when all the windows were covered with blackout curtains. She'd met
him in this very room, the shy millionaire who doubled
his fortune every single month by trading with pirates
and all the Axis powers.

"Where's my little girl?"

"She's not your girl. I raised her."

"Where is she?"

"With the Frog."

He started to groan.

"Stop that," she said. "You knew where I was taking
her. That was part of the deal."

"He's a bumper."

"And what are you?"

"A philanthropist."

She laughed, and he couldn't keep up with her moves
on the floor. "I don't go around socking people in the
head."

"You do much worse. You steal their lives and make
them suffer. Holden puts them out of their misery."

"Go ahead. Congratulate Sid. Is he living at Aladdin?"

"Stop it, Howard. You know where he is."

"On the island? On Chappy? With that maniac, Ethan
Cardinale? Ethan killed Kronstadt, for Christ's sake."

"You killed her, old man."

He was blubbering now, under the mad pull of the
horns. Judith could have jumped out the window.

"I didn't strangle Kronstadt."

"Yes you did. Ethan was only your twin. Didn't you tell me that?"

He stopped dancing. And the orchestra stopped. They could have been at Versailles, or some other house of kings . . . and little queens like Marie Antoinette. He danced. He stopped. And the music was like a telegraph machine.

"He's your twin."

"He's a fucking miser and a maniac. He'd have eaten his own mama for a dollar bill. But I won't bother Ethan and the Frog if you stay with me."

"I promised, old man. Didn't I promise?"

"I want it in writing," Howard said, truculent and sad.

"Your lawyer or mine?"

"No lawyers."

"Then what would you like?"

"A note," he said.

"Right now? While we're dancing?"

"After the dance. I'm not so particular. You'll have to swear on your life that you'll live with me."

"Howard, I'll haunt you worse than Kronstadt ever did. Kronstadt will feel like afternoon tea."

"It don't matter . . . long as you're mine."

"I'll make you dance morning, noon, and night."

"It don't matter. I have the orchestra. I have the men . . . but I gotta know. When is my daughter coming to stay with us?"

"She's not coming. She has the Frog."

"Jesus, his dad was my chauffeur."

"And Frog is president of Aladdin. That's America, old man."

She led Howard over the floor, his shoes like an

anchor that kept her from flying into some glass. She'd been suicidal since she was ten. Was she born with that need to hurt herself? Is that what Howard adored? Suicide in the way she danced.

"Sid can't have her," he said.

Judith stopped dancing. The trombones were caught in the middle of a cry. The waiters hovered close, in case Howard happened to fall.

"I'll leave you, old man. This is the last dance we'll ever have."

"I'll cut you off without a cent."

"I'm glad. I'll go to Chappaquiddick. I'll sponge off Ethan. I'll live with Ethan Cardinale."

"Ethan? I'll break his neck. You can't win." Then he started to wail. "Dance with me, Judith. I'm getting cold."

His whole body was shaking, and she gathered up Howard in her arms, like a bag of bones dressed in green. She'd devoted half a century to this old man.

"I won't have Sid as my son-in-law."

"Yes you will."

And they went round and round the floor. She could almost see a rooster in the chandeliers. The horns crowed at her. It felt like midnight. She was dancing with Howard Phipps.